Leaflings
A Prequel

The Raising of the Amethyst Stone

Darren Shell

PUBLISHED BY FIDELI PUBLISHING

ISBN: 978-1-955622-27-1

Fideli Publishing

Martinsville, IN, USA

Cover by Fideli Publishing

Cover art by: MarsOhod via stock.adobe.com

Other Works by the Author

Fiction

Leaflings: A Triligoy (also available in audio book)

Street Smart

Lost Treasure

The Angel's Share

Death Wish

No Safety Bars and Other Stories
(A Compilation of Short Stories)

Graveyard Tour

The Old Lady of the Lake

Nonfiction

The History of Dale Hollow Lake

Stories from Dale Hollow
(Short Stories, Pictures, and History of Dale Hollow Lake and The Obey River Valley)

A Stone's Throw
(The History of the Game of Marbles
In Tennessee and Kentucky)

The Big Ones
(The World Record Smallmouth Bass
Of Dale Hollow Lake)

Against Heavy Odds
(From Backyard to Champion
The Eddie Swanson Story)

Leaflings

A Prequel

The Raising of the Amethyst Stone

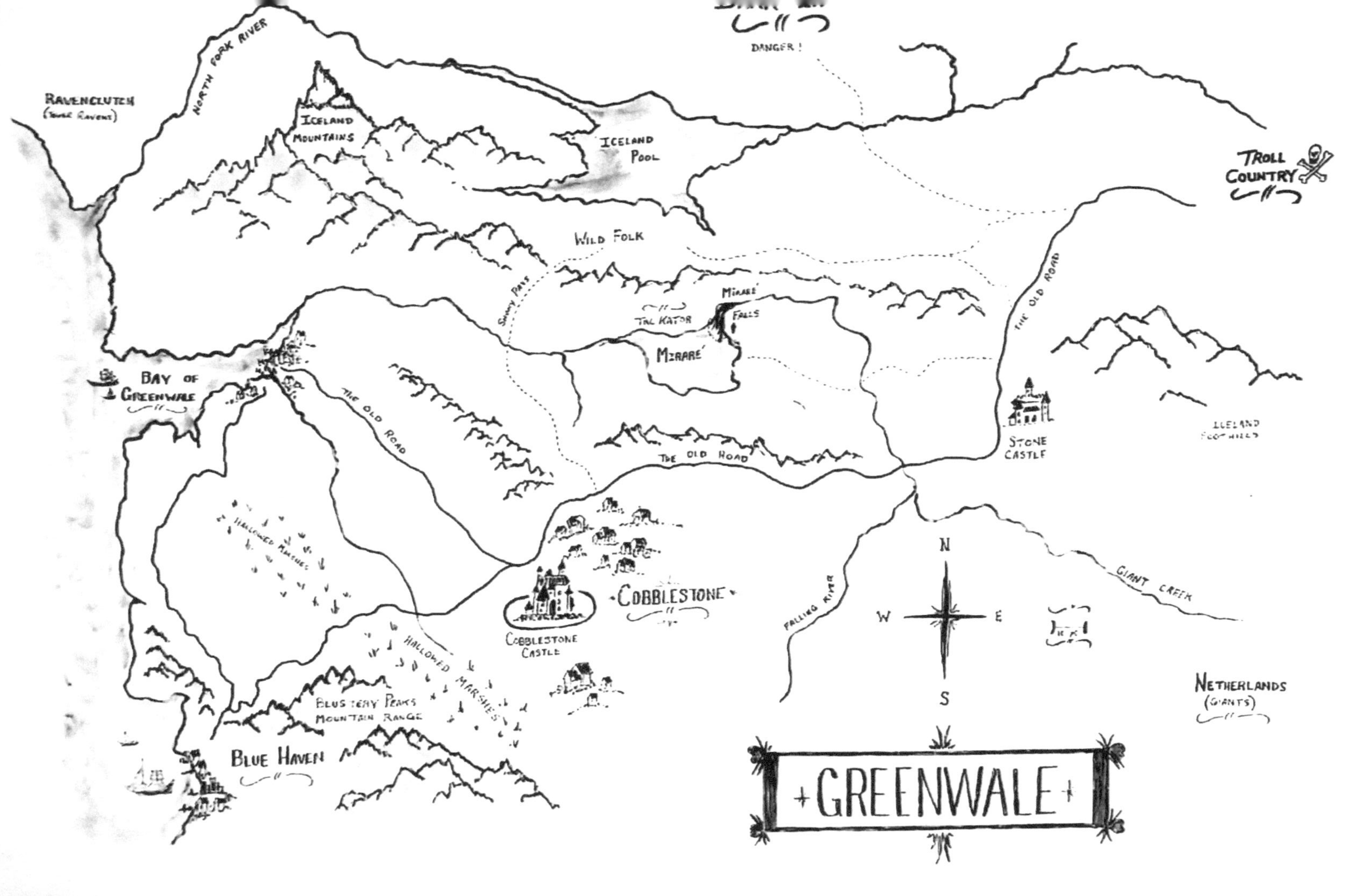
GREENWALE
Ravenclutch
North Fork River
Iceland Mountains
Iceland Pool
Danger!
Troll Country
Wild Folk
Tal Kator
Mirare' Falls
Mirare'
The Old Road
Stone Castle
Iceland Foothills
Bay of Greenwale
The Old Road
The Old Road
Hallowed Marshes
Hallowed Marshes
Cobblestone
Cobblestone Castle
Falling River
Giant Creek
N
W
E
S
Blustery Peaks Mountain Range
Blue Haven
Netherlands (Giants)

From "The Lay of the Amethyst Stone"
The Age of Enlightenment

From fiery night it fell
As if from burning Hell.
It scorched into the ground
To places still unfound.
And from disaster came
Life without a name.

They pulled their roots from land
And walked on foot and hand.
And raised by human fist
Came the Shard of Amethyst.

... and the Prequel Begins

1

Midsummers Eve

The light of a nearly full moon glistened on the newly fashioned slate shingles of Stone Castle. The sparkling dew twinkled on the hand-hewn rock walls jutting toward the midnight sky full of stars. Clean, new tapestries danced in the open windows above the now completed rock statue of a building of some ten years in its construction. The scent of honeysuckle filled the night air and crickets chirped their soothing midsummer tune. The Deep Forest was quiet, and all seemed well in this wooded domain as ten aged men sat quietly around the dwindling embers of the fire pit beneath the looming tower above. Only the glow of the fire lit the courtyard as well as the faces of these silent men circled in deep thought. Their solemn hearts did not mirror the serenity that surrounded them.

These were men of importance. These ten were the eldest of perhaps forty-five males that considered this place home. A handful of temporary residents stayed here as well, being younger men, who either by their own accord, or were placed here by the promptings of their families seeking to school their son in the wise teachings of these special men. Some others were those that chose to visit periodically for brief periods of time, steering their travels here for a few weeks or months in succession. Creed or color made no difference within these walls; only that the heart of the man must have the same focus as the rest who resided here.

That topic, or state of mind, was *enlightenment.*

These ten men around the fire were the council that governed this group who fancied to ponder the wonders of the world that have both plagued and entertained mankind since the dawn of time. All, in their previous lives, had been men of stature, learned and successful entrepreneurs in one walk of life or another. Some were great agriculturalists. Most were scholars or philanthropists or even astronomers that felt they had derived all the satisfaction they could from their careers and/or family lives. Men of strength. Men of means. Men of intelligence. Men of POWER … all now quietly living in near solitude, reading volumes of literature and meditating.

These were the *Literati.* They were revered … even feared. They were renowned far and wide. They were often sought for counsel by kings and queens, giving input to architects building castles much like the one that housed this remarkably intelligent group of individuals.

Their solitude and secrecy alone kept most of the outside world from venturing to that special spot in the Deep Forest. Their boundaries were not manned or guarded, mostly because there was little need of such. Commoners were intimidated by the heir of prowess emitted by the Literati. Councilmen, royalty and others of higher society respectfully only entered their realm on direct and intentional purpose.

To some, their ways were that of eerie wizards or warlocks, but such was not the case. In all actuality, this group of men were generally kind of heart, but cautiously wise with a sense of higher status toward all. Any humble heart could enter but would not likely be received with hospitable favor. One could state one's business, then be expected to move along swiftly.

So, perception of the Literati failed to reflect the fact that they were, in fact, quite noble at heart and did have the world's best interests at their forefront. Their understandings of the delicate balance of nature versus mankind's intrusion were quite intriguing. They strove to find balance in all things, especially those complexities that could affect or influence the future for good or evil. Unfortunately, good and evil are also sometimes a matter of prospective.

The Literati managed to build this wondrous Stone Castle using natural stone harvested in the least harmful way so as not to affect the balance of the forest. Their roads were merely paths, sometimes overgrown … sometimes heavily trodden, then allowed to grow back over again into rough and woody terrain. Even their water supply was supplied by a small trench, hand dug from the nearby river (that would one day be named The Falling River). The trench wound delicately through the wooded terrain, through gravel flats (to help purify), meticulously covered in flat stone, and then eventually tumble onto the masoned stone creek channel running beneath the castle. It was a work of art and engineering. It rarely froze in winter and supplied the castle with just enough water to fulfill its needs without hindering nature in any way.

A rarely viewed trait of nearly all of the Literati was their practice of occasionally spending a three-day personal sabbatical in the forest where they would bring no food or water and would fast, all the while being mostly still and silent, taking in their surroundings … achieving a Zen-like state in which to meditate.

When not fasting, most would spend waking hours poring over the castle's lavish library of hand-scribed, leather-bound volumes of literature. Such a wealth of information was housed within those walls. No such library could rival it. It, in and of itself, was perhaps more valuable than the grand castle that housed it.

And then, there were the *debates*. Weekly, the Literati would cluster into small groups or round tables to openly discuss grand ideas or to ponder seemingly insignificant recent events that meant something of importance to them. There was no end to their lists of topics for debate. One full council was once given to the topic of a pack of wolves that had relocated away from their section of the wood to another. Although nothing could be done to change it, every rat and snail was given equal thought. Deep subjects seemed to be fancied the most, such as fazes of the moon in relation to wave patterns in the tides of the Bay of Greenwater. Astrology was perhaps the most heavily pondered and viewed subject matter.

Such was tonight's topic, and it was of extreme importance. Volumes of unspoken information were racing through the minds of these spiritual men as they sat in total silence, each lost in their own thoughts.

The crickets still chirped. The fireflies still shown against the darkness. The embers of fire dwindled further. The world's brightest men continued to worry.

* * *

The awkward silence was broken by the heavy boot steps emerging from the castle.

From the silent halls of the castle onto the equally quiet courtyard stone, the tall and strong stature of a man stepped toward the group of Literati. His appearance seemed out of place amongst these robed and cloaked elders. His stately leather long-coat was tightly cinched by a thick leather belt. His tall boots reached high beneath his coat, and his wide-brimmed hat shadowed his weathered and darkened skin. He looked pirate-ish, and in all likelihood, he perhaps was. He'd sailed many seas and came here as often as possible when in port at the Bay of Greenwale. He was well-known amid these men, although his demeanor was nothing like anyone who'd ever stayed at Stone Castle.

He cared not of the celibacy these men abided for themselves, which probably attested to his sometimes-long absence. Celibacy was not a prerequisite at Stone Castle, but many of these scholars seemed to have lost that part of their lives to but mere memory. He walked near to the fire and stood in silence along with them.

His name in his native tongue was Sharique (pronounced with a roll of the tongue at the R), but for obvious reasons, he was known by most as Shark. His ethnicity was known only to him, and he resembled no one else in physique or character. His accent was strange to them, but his verbiage was quite intelligent and even soothing at times for such a burly fellow. He decided to break the silence.

"It takes no scholar to detect such intense and foreboding thought." His words were gentle and delivered with respect and subtlety. He knew them all well enough to speak freely, but he could easily tell that there was much more to this picture than first glance. He spoke again.

"I suspect your personal thoughts are overflowing within. Might I be included in the knowledge that weighs so heavily upon you all?"

Elias was the usual spokesperson of this group, and he had a well-preserved friendship with his friend he called Shark. Elias spoke.

"I fear you shall hear more than you care to know. 'Tis a weight of worry."

Shark nestled himself onto the cool stone floor, staring intently toward Elias. He patiently waited as the old man before him gathered his words.

"Have you not seen the southern sky?"

Shark nodded, still silent.

"We have a new star, brilliant and beautiful."

"That sounds like a good thing," Shark whispered, almost beneath his voice.

"No," sighed Elias. "No, it is not. Such a thing has not happened in this age. None of us have ever witnessed such, but the passed-down tales and documentations of our forefathers share our worry. For us

... for us, it is for now a beautiful elusion shining ever so brightly like a beacon from Heaven. From our sight glass, we can discern the hint of a glorious white tail flailing from behind—it, too, seeming like the splendors of the gods are about to be bestowed upon us. And make no mistake ... **it's coming here.**"

Shark's eyes widened into saucers. His trembling voice cracked as it pierced the night air ...

"That is no star ...
"It's a meteor."

2

The Deep Forest was a very large and somewhat uncharted menagerie of jutting cliffs, valleys of ancient hardwoods, acres of swamp lands choked with wild grasses and flowers, as well as a number of small lakes each fed by numerous creeks and tiny rivers. Its beauty was breathtaking. Many of its creature inhabitants were still unknown, and still other beasts were better left unfound. But even with its impending dangers, the richness of these many acres was a glory to behold. Precious animals and human species rejoiced in its bountiful abundance. Each plant and animal coincided with one another, sometimes ferociously … sometimes lovingly.

In a section of this great forest, lived a colony of special people. They were very much human, but they had lived for so long in the wild that many of their mannerisms seemed far less human than one might think. They had originally left a township of man called Cobblestone, abandoning their livelihood for a life away from the bustle of the city. They traversed many miles into the Great Forest crossing the snowy peak known simply as Iceland. It was but one lone mountain just tall enough to carry a snowy peak most of the season. This band of folk felt safe with this distance between them and the city folk they called "Cobblers". No one among them could fully remember the reasonings of their ancestors to abandon Cobblestone and that way of life, but all still carried a distaste for outsiders of any kind, especially from that city. They kept tightly to their creed of wildland people and were fiercely loyal to their individual families, which they called pods. They had little need for last names, but for the sake of simplicity, each pod was referred to as where they lived in the colony. There were the Riverpools, Lowlanders, Branchers (known to live in the trees), and Rockies. Many other similar nicknames were given them as well.

This band of people were mostly of three large families that were relatively close of kin. So, as time marched on and the group procreated for future survival, it was only natural for the whole group to take on most of the same characteristics and traits and demeanors.

For instance, all of them have jet black hair well into their fifties and sixties (if they live that long in the wild). Their large dark eyes see well in the nighttime. They were shorter and thinner than most of Cobblestone's citizens and were far more agile. They could shimmy a tree in seconds and carry twice their weight over their heads for long distances. They were particularly apt at wielding bamboo staffs as weapons, practicing the art in any spare moments. Their skin was darker than the paler skinnier Cobblestone citizens, and they wore very little clothing.

They did, however, wear blanket-like cloaks woven out of marsh grasses, leaves, and twigs. Their shoes were makeshift sandals woven out of the same substance. They sometimes dyed these coverings with berry juices and mud to aid in the camouflage. That was its only purpose … to disguise themselves from danger. In their eyes, any other walk of life was dangerous, and keeping hidden was their solution to survival.

In times of need, they would be forced to travel to the city of Cobblestone to trade goods with a handful of individuals they deemed safe enough to barter goods. A spokesperson would don a vague semblance of clothing, while another dozen or so would travel along to help carry the load of goods to be traded.

There was little these people had to trade with the rest of the outside world. They had found that the people of Cobblestone fancied wild mushrooms and a particular type of nut that only grew in their section of the forest. Also, a variety of tree growing there had remarkably straight branches that could be fashioned into great arrows for the Cobblestone men's longbows. These types of goods would be carried across the mountain and traded for dried fruits, and in some special cases, dried meats. Meat was but a small part of their diet, but they knew that it was good for the strength of their bodies and would partake, especially in the cold of winter when little else was available other than their foraged nuts, scant few fish from The Iceland Pool, and snails from the river. Their snails were quite a delicacy for them, but a winter's worth grew old quickly. Some of what Cobblestone had to offer was most welcome when food became scarce.

Most of Cobblestone's citizens considered these woodland folk barbaric and unkempt. They smelled of woods and campfires and did most of their bathing in the warmer months. For them, this seemed perfectly natural, but the townsfolk cared little for it. Cobblestone called them "The Wild Folk", and the name stuck.

The term Wild Folk was not a fully fitting assessment of these remarkable people. Although they lived in the wild and were very much in tune with the creatures of the forest, they still did manage to maintain intelligent speech and talked much like the town of Cobblestone. Some of their own slang had worked its way into their communications with one another, but their language skills were still quite sharp. Speech and schooling came from the parents and grandparents of the youngsters from an early age. This also kept the family bond exceptionally close, full of love and respect. They had become very apt at planting beautiful gardens of vegetables, cleverly sown around the other forest plants, and all who lived here shared of love of things that blossom, grow, and bear fruit.

So, the term Wild Folk did not fit in this regard—but if an outsider trespassed or offended in any way, the Wild Folk were very much Wild. They had become fierce with the wielding of bamboo sticks for protection and could hold their own with most any walk of life, especially when the pods banded together. It kept their village dangerous to outsiders and safe for themselves.

Their section of woods was full of booby traps and snares to ensure protection of the pods and also give alerts to possible incoming danger. When someone or something tripped one of their sensors, a frenzied rush passed through the camp immediately. Within thirty seconds, there was no trace of them at all, save perhaps a campfire. Their camouflage made them disappear as they watched and listened.

On this day, Lilly Riverpool, the sixteen-year-old daughter of loving parents was searching for snails in the water's edge with her mother.

"Momma," asked Lilly. "Why do we hate the Cobblers?"

"Hate is a harsh word, Lilly," her mother replied.

"But we don't like 'em none, though, right?"

"Poor grammar, Lilly. *Don't like them much*, she corrected.

"Yeah, that's what I mean," Lilly stated again. "What makes them so bad?"

"Because they are not like us, and that's all you need to know about them," her mother offered. "They are meddlesome and unfriendly. We don't like them."

Lilly was not satisfied with that answer. "What about the Literati?" she then asked.

"They are rich," stated her mother, "and extra smart and they think they are better than us. We don't like them either," was her mother's reply.

"If they *are* that smart, maybe they are better than us."

"Nonsense, little lady. Everybody has to be something, and we are what we are. Far as I'm concerned, WE are better than those snooty old men."

"So, it's okay if we think we are better than them, but it's not nice for them to think the same of us?" Lilly could sense she'd touched a nerve.

"Dig your snails, missy! Enough with the questions!"

"But …"

"NO BUTS!"

Lilly chuckled out loud. "They have no butts, Momma?"

"Lord, child, you wear me out!"

Aside from Lilly's excessive chatterings and questions throughout the day, her family thought of her as a true gift from Heaven. She had been a blessing when they needed it most.

A month before Lilly was born, her older brother of six years of age, suddenly died of a snake bite. He'd been playing on the rock bluffs overlooking the lake when his cry came out. All rushed to the six-year-old crying in shock, but it was of no avail. Two days later his heart stopped as his parents held him in their arms in utter tears.

It was a devastating blow for Lilly's parents to have lost their first born. For a month they wandered aimlessly around camp sobbing, their eyes distant and sorrowful. Some said her mother would never give birth with such sadness in her heart. She wasn't eating and she drew away from everyone, even her husband, who was battling his own sorrows of pain and remembrance.

But that's when Lilly came along. The pain of birth was a different pain, and it seemed to shake Lilly's mother back into reality. Her husband soon followed suit and once again looked forward to the new days ahead with this precious little girl that was their saving grace. They named her Lilly, after the wondrous flowers around the water where they lived. Lilly grew and flourished and became just as lovely as her namesake. (If you don't ask a Cobbler).

For as long as she could remember, she felt her happiest near the water. She loved the sounds and smells water would offer her. She found true comfort living where she did, where woods and water met. It wasn't just home. It was more than that. At times, she thought she could almost hear a voice in the currents when all was quiet. The gentle drippings were notes of song to her ears. She felt a special connection both in and near water's edge. The notes she heard were as if someone was gently plucking the strings of a harp in the distance, and the vibrations echoed into her chest with warmth and purity. She called it her rainbow within, and it stayed with her forever.

Lilly still had questions for her mother and was growing impatient with the partial answers she was receiving. She spoke up again.

"Here in our home … our people … some are not as nice as others. Some are mean at times. Some are smarter than others. Some climb trees or swim better. Some don't communicate as well."

"Yes, child. What is your point?"

"Don't you think that these other people could be the same way? Are we judging all by the actions of a few?"

Lilly was wise beyond her years. Few noticed. Even she would have trouble grasping this fact. She was special. She had honed her heart and mind to feel the forest and waters of home. She had unknowingly studied others in her village. She was a star gazer and a student of life—and it showed in the way she lived. She wanted to experience more than just the shores of the Iceland Pool. In her mind, she was preparing to travel. One lone girl with a huge heart was about to embark on the journey of her lifetime.

And little did she know—that the love and compassion in her heart … would one day … alter the fate—of all.

The early evening sky in Cobblestone was still showing its faint oranges and reds, turning to deep purple. Star gazing was a pastime here practiced by many. Most of the rooftops had a window that stepped out onto the roofs. It was an inexpensive pastime, and it was a comfort to many of all ages.

The hot topic around town was this new and beautiful star that had only just arrived in the sky a night or two before. It was the talk of the town. Its sighting was making ordinary lives more extraordinary.

Inside the mote and tall walls of Cobbletone Castle, this story was unfolding in a much different way. King Marcus, Queen Laura, the royal council, and a large number of soldiers were holding a stressful meeting in the castle's Council Hall. King Marcus spoke aloud.

"My council, I'm certain you are all in understanding of the magnitude of this meeting. Let me remind you of your oaths of secrecy in this matter. The townspeople are enjoying this new star in the evening sky. There is no need for widespread panic. As you know, the meteor will either miss us or kill us all. That much we have no control over; nor do they. This matter is to be kept in utter secrecy. All in understanding?"

"Your Highness," asked a councilman. "What options do we have? This is hit or miss, correct?"

"Our options, Sir Stephen, are in the aftermath." The king turned his attention toward the crowd. "Henceforward, we will operate under the assumption that we will survive impact. We must increase food supplies in the North, South, and East Farthings, as well as here in the castle. In the event of a partial hit, some of our reserves may be saved in separation. We will also prepare the castle's lower halls as shelter if necessity arises. What we do in the castle will be easily concealed. Our work in the other farthings will have to be done with more care as not to cause suspicion."

The king paused to let the information set in and then continued. "Furthermore," he continued, "if there is impact in nearby realms other than our own, those of us in this room will be expected to make haste to assess damages elsewhere. Each of you will create a list of others to assist you. You will keep this list secret until further notice. You will only contact those on the list after impact. Communicate only with one another in this room, comparing lists so that all will hopefully have fire-fighters, medicine men, and other caretakers. Plan for additional horses from the citizens of town if possible.

"I have sent Tower Ravens to Stone Castle requesting information and perhaps advice. The Literati are wise and have historical documentation in their libraries that could shed light on any possible occurrences in our history. They've been sworn to secrecy as well. The birds have yet to return. I will advise when that happens."

After a number of questions fielded from the crowd, the king called the meeting adjourned. He then motioned for his two closest advisors to join him secretly down a nearby corridor. Quietly and mischievously, he addressed them.

"Men, assuming we survive, there will be a secondary mission implemented as well. I've consulted our library on this subject as well. There were two minor meteor hits in our documented history. On each of these occurrences, the extreme heat in the ground after impact did something very special. It changed the composition of the bedrock beneath the surface. The burning of ore and belching of steam manipulate the soil and stones. Once cooled, it will be time for us to search for them."

With wry smiles, both men raised an eyebrow and spoke in unison.

"Search for what?"

The king's eerie grin was accompanied by a quiet chuckle.

"Jewels!"

4

By early morning, the gathering of men in Stone Castle's courtyard had disbanded, save one.

Still alongside the now-cold embers of last night's fire, sat an anciently old man. His green hooded cloak was still drawn over his head, and both fists were gripped into midair in front him. He rocked back and forth with rhythmic gyrations. His body lightly trembled, and his closed eyes darted back and forth in his head. Semi-consciously he was wrestling something in his mind.

His name was Tolk. Famed far and wide for his foretellings as a prophet and wise man, his reputation was unquestioned everywhere he went. Through his last two decades, he found himself in the seclusion of this group of men, speaking and writing countless books—ever trying to document both history and the special prophesies that plagued his brilliant mind. Some said he was tormented. Some said blessed. But regardless, when the Great Tolk spoke, all listened.

Tolk had spent many years of his earlier life working for kings and influential people scribing ancient literature for vast libraries, making copies of priceless books on history, philosophy, physics, and even prophesy. As he scribed, he learned and became wise beyond wise. The more he learned, the more the voices in his head pounded to get out. He was paid well for his services over the years, so when he chose early retirement from these tedious jobs of scribing, most knew the real reason for his leaving.

He was mentally unstable.

Mentally stable or not, he was immeasurably wise. His fellow Literati could not often get through to him, and when they did, he would either dismiss them or unleash an enormous amount of information on whatever the subject matter was. No one dared ask Tolk a question without having pen and parchment in hand. The answers would flow like water over a waterfall—the asker attempting to catch it in buckets.

He often spoke and wrote in rhythmic rhyme. Sometimes whole chapters of eerie prophesy flowed with beautiful rhyming lyric. This only added to its mystery. Though sometimes misconstrued, his prophesies were always right if one could view them from the correct vantage point.

There were still other times during his writings that strange scratching art would be scribbled onto a page. It would look like nothing to the naked eye up close, but viewed from across the room, from one direction or another, the subject could be clearly viewed. It was three-dimensional drawing created from a different vantage point from its intended viewing.

Countless other idiosyncrasies swirled within this man's mind. The other Literati knew to steer clear of him if one of his episodes took place … much like the one happening on this day.

Still Tolk rocked back and forth in the courtyard.

He woke with a start. He gained his senses as if waking from a long nap. Soon, though, the topics in his daydreams were coming to his conscious mind, and with them came a weight that strained the old man.

Instantly, he tore open the book that filled his lap and scrambled for his ink and pen. Without even a sip of water after twelve hours of mental confinement, Tolk started filling his pages as quickly as his antique fingers could scribble. With a solitary grunt, his prophesy began.

Through fiery night it fell, as if from burning Hell …

* * *

Within the halls of Stone Castle, the rest of the Literati were gathering in the council hall. Elias took the stand.

"Men, I assume you all now know why this meeting has been called. We do, in fact, have a meteor on its way. We have no idea what size it is, and we have no conclusions about where it may land. It could be leagues from here, but it very well could be here as well. We have little to go on but the old writings of the past and our gut feelings."

A young man of seventeen years of age was standing in the back corner with numerous questions on his mind, not willing to speak up just yet. His name was Daniel. Here on his own accord, his family paid dearly to get the Literati to agree to let him stay here in the castle and learn from the many great minds that shared time in this special location.

Daniel had grown up inquisitive and delved into literature at a young age. By age twelve, he had devoured virtually every book of lore in his hometown libraries in the city known as Blue Haven along the shores of the Green Sea. Many leagues from Stone Castle, far south of Cobblestone, he made the journey in six days, packing his belongings over the mountain range called Blustery Peaks and then down along the Hallowed Marshes south of Cobblestone. He stocked up his provisions on his way through Cobblestone, finishing the remaining day's trip to Stone Castle thereafter. Every step for him was fulfilling—exhilarating perhaps. He was eager to learn as well as excited to see new landscapes and people he'd never seen before. He considered his journey priceless, although his parents probably thought differently, given the cost of this education. A strong-willed and good-hearted young man, his presence was welcomed by the Literati.

Blue Haven had but one small castle, and it housed a small brood of Tower Ravens that aided in communication between cities and Stone Castle. All of Daniel's specifics were set up long before he arrived, thanks to the special efforts of those magnificent birds, the Tower Ravens. Afterall, it was the Literati that first bread and raised the ravens and taught them to speak. Many of the birds understood an abundance of words spoken to them, and most could speak a number of words to some degree. The ravens were beyond valuable and proved their worth daily.

Daniel finally spoke up. "Sir Elias?" he asked. "Where shall we help study … to find answers?"

"Patience, Master Daniel," replied Elias. "We've studied every piece of literature we have, finding little. Our efforts now would be better suited planning for the aftermath should we survive initial impact. No one knows what repercussions will follow thereafter."

"There must be something we can do," stated Shark, quiet up until now.

Elias continued. "We are putting together a small band of volunteers for the quest for answers after impact and stabilization. The elders will not be able to make this trek. We will need three able-bodied men, seasoned enough for rough travel. We will be sending Talc, our eldest Raven. The party will be instructed on how best to use him to send word back to us for evaluation."

"I volunteer!" called Daniel, his hand raised high.

"I was counting on you, Master Daniel," replied Elias. "You are strong of might and strong of will. Who else shall go?"

Shark raised his hand.

The third to volunteer was an acquaintance of Daniel's. The two had become fast friends, having arrived at Stone Castle in the same month of spring, earlier this year. His name was Claybon, a rather sharp lad with a fiery demeanor. His placement at Stone Castle was not of his own liking, being sent here from Cobblestone by his father, the local blacksmith, urging his son off to schooling. His father wanted more for his son than the sweat and grime he had toiled in during his early years. Though more than intelligent enough to study with the Literati, Claybon would probably have been quite happy in a hands-on job much like his father. He was a little heavy-set and remarkably strong for his age of eighteen. He had fancied a plan of working in the shipyard in the Bay of Greenwale, hearing tall tales told by the incoming seamen from leagues away as he fashioned side-board planks from rare woods from far away forests. Alas, he was at Stone Castle, and he was happy to volunteer for something away from here, even if it meant unknown danger and intrigue. His floppy red hair nodded as he raised his hand.

Those three men made up the band for the journey, whenever that day arrived.

Elias accepted the volunteers and continued. "In the meantime, we must gather firewood and fill the stone shelter. If the forest is burned, we will still need fire to boil water and cook. Others may gather nuts for the lower pantries. Mushrooms will be of little avail. We need food we can preserve for weeks, even months. Hunters, we need Elk for salting. We must fill far more crocks with fresh water than usual. Our water supply may be compromised."

The crowd was making mental notes and comparing tasks to their own skillsets.

Elias' next comment was unsettling.

"Make sure each of you has some means of protection. We need stones, bamboo, anything that could be used as a weapon. If we are the only ones with food, others will come for it. Let us hope it isn't trolls."

Shark looked over to Daniel, who was still grasping at that last sentence. With a raised eyebrow, he whispered, "Big rocks."

If only big rocks were all they would need.

5

"Momma," Lilly said quietly, "we need to talk."

"Oh, what is it now, child?" her mother asked. "I don't know why the sky is blue or the water green."

"I'm serious, Momma. I want to travel." Lilly's eyes were sincere.

"TRAVEL?" she cried. "Why in the world would you want to do such a thing?! It's dangerous out there, especially for a young lady as yourself! The world is no place for you!"

"I'm very serious, Momma. The world IS a place for me. I want to see it. I want to see Cobblestone, and maybe Stone Castle."

"Lord, child! How would you defend yourself? What would you eat? You have no money for the city. It's ridiculous! I won't have it!"

"Momma, Poppa has taught me skill with the bamboo. I can defend myself. I can barter with what I bring with me. I feel as if I've learned what this village has to offer. I want to see what's out there—good and bad. I want this."

"We will NOT allow it!" her mother cried.

"I'd much rather have your blessing when I go, Momma."

"The answer is no." Tears fell from her mother's eyes as she thought of her only daughter leaving the pod, if only for a short while.

"Then I'm asking Poppa."

* * *

"Absolutely not!" shouted her father. "There are far more dangers out there than I can even tell you about. There are cave trolls and mountain trolls. There are dastardly men in the cities that could … could … I shudder to think of it. Not with your own band of soldiers would this be good. You mustn't go, sweetheart."

"Poppa. I've thought about this for a long time. I've wanted it for almost as long. There is a new star in the sky, Poppa. New and exciting. I'm taking it as a sign that this is my time to live and learn. I long to travel and see other peoples, even if it is unpleasant."

"My daughter. I fear that *unpleasant* is the least of what you will experience. What if you never came home? How could your mother and I cope? What about your little brother?"

"All of you will be here when I return, Poppa. I'm not going forever. I love it here. I will return. I just need to see, Poppa, or I will never forgive myself for settling for a lackluster life."

"Lilly," her father whimpered, tears flowing, "I cannot in good conscience allow this. It is folly!"

"I really wanted your blessing, Poppa. You've taught me well the art of bamboo. I can protect myself. I will have food. I will taste other foods, meet new people. The new moon will find me back here, if not before. Perhaps I will hate the journey, but I will not hate it as much as never taking the leap of faith to make it. I will return by the new moon, or before if it becomes too much for me. You have my word."

"Lilly, you will look dreadfully out of place. Their ways are not like ours. You will be lost." His voice trailed off into silent tears as he staired into the morning sky as if that star could somehow be seen in the light.

"You've never been, Poppa. Neither did your father. We don't know how bad or how good it can be." She paused, searching for more words. With little more she could say, she uttered the last words her father wanted to hear. "I'm leaving in the morning. I love you, Poppa."

Her father only wept, knowing full well the mannerisms of his little girl—her head-strong, fervent ways. He knew that before she completed her first sentence, but it did not mend his heart in the least. This girl was his gift from God, and that gift would no doubt be walking away for the first time in sixteen years of life. His heart melted, as if her words were forever, her actions unchangeable. For him, it seemed as if the greatest song was about to end, leaving him with only silence. Sadness overwhelmed him.

Lilly pulled him into strong embrace, crying as she squeezed tighter. Eventually, she pulled away and left disheartened and sad, yet still very much determined to fulfill what she considered her destiny, especially now that she had her own new star to guide her.

That mysterious new star was tugging at many eyes and hearts, but Lilly's heart was the only one happy about it. All that glitters, is not gold, but soon she would be off to find the glitter, whatever that glitter might be.

* * *

News spread through the village in an instant. The awkward silence of foreboding worry took hold with friends and family having few words to share in what would usually be deemed unthinkable among these pods. Aside from Lilly's parents, the news was perhaps hardest for her younger brother. He was at the delicate age of seven, where so many "givens" in life are just taking root in the mind. He was unquestionably close to Lilly, and life without her near every day seemed unfathomable. She had made the sandals he wore daily. It was she that taught him how to dig for snails along the riverbanks. She was very motherly to him, teaching him many new words of speech, and telling him nighttime stories before sleep. He tagged along most days as she gathered the mosses and grasses for weaving clothing. He loved how she talked about the water and how it would sing to her when she listened. Young Kato would be lost without her.

By morning, Lilly had woven three large pouches for carrying her provisions, which were scant. She had a large bundle of plump snails packed in one pouch and carried another pouch empty in hopes of finding mushrooms along the way. With her, she would carry her strongest bamboo shaft to use as a walking stick, hoping to never draw it up in defense. One end of the stick was sharpened around the edge, designed for severe damage if a situation presented itself. She prayed no altercation such as that would ever happen. She was very apt at using the staff, sparring with her father and friends ferociously, but a real foe was something she'd never experienced.

She wished that she had some sort of way to document her travels. Though very lingual and articulated in speech, the Wild Folk did not read or write. They counted on pictures scratched on stone or wood as their form of historical documentation. These hieroglyphics were all around their village, but parchment was not available to them. Pen and ink were foreign to them. She would simply have to remember her travels and share them with future generations, just as it had been done for decades before her.

Saying goodbye would perhaps be the hardest part of her journey. It seemed no matter how badly she wished to go, the love of her family was a mainstay she'd sorely miss. In the end, the enticement of the trail ahead outweighed the tugging of her heartstrings but pulling away from Kato was tearing her heart out. He just couldn't grasp the concept of her leaving and returning.

Lilly's mother was desperately trying to show her distaste in her leaving, but all that she could muster was a teary "I love you so much." Her warm hug was a long one.

Her father very nearly let her go without saying goodbye. He simply could not fathom her reasoning for leaving their placid shores. It seemed every emotion he'd ever felt was crushing inward on him. He, too, finally pulled away from her hug. In his hand was a rolled-up piece of leather made of sewn together rabbit hides. It looked extremely old and discolored as if it had been stowed away for a long period of time. He handed it to her and spoke, "Perhaps this will help. I couldn't read the words, but the pictures might help you some."

Lilly unrolled what her father had given her. On the inside of the leather cloth, an elaborate map had been penned. Pictures of mountains and streams were scrolled across its surface with lettering she could not understand but could easily tell the lines of different pathways leading to castles and bodies of water.

"It was my great-grandfather's," her father explained. "I never thought I'd have a need for it until now. I hope it serves you well."

"Poppa, thank you!" Lilly choked back the tears and she caressed the maps surface. "I think it will do nicely."

"Take the Snowy Pass south over the mountain. Travel only by day, and do not tarry on the pass. Foul things come down from the Iceland Peak. When you cross the Falling River in the valley below, the path winds westward. That is your trail. From there, I don't know anything of it. Stick closely to it and hide from any altercations. Best be secret until you make your entrance into Cobblestone. You will look very much out of place in town in your woven cloak. You will need to obtain some semblance of clothing somehow. There are a thousand things I can't prepare you for. I pray the Lord will guide you and care for your well-being. I love you, my child. Please be safe."

With that, he quickly turned and walked away, never looking back as she began her journey. He didn't want her to see the tears he could no longer hold back. He pretended to be tough, but Tucker was a softy when it came to family. He, too, was lost, even before her feet took a step.

With a final glance across the village and a wave to hundreds of staring eyes, Lilly set her sights on the mountain that lie in front of her. Relieved that the goodbyes were complete, a wide smile crossed her face.

"Onward and upward, Lilly Girl," she told herself. "New worlds are not found over calm seas." She couldn't remember where she'd heard that term, but it seemed to fit the occasion. She'd certainly never seen the sea, but someday hoped to make that journey as well. But for now, it was just her and this mountain path. "Upward," she said again.

After only a few steps, Lilly paused in her tracks. She felt the water behind her and heard that familiar sound in her head that she knew so well. It was that delicate water-harp teasing the butterflies in her stomach. She hoped the forest would have streams that sang to her like the shores of The Iceland Pool. She would carry that feeling with her on this journey. If nothing on this trip would be familiar to her, that love of water would be her comfort in strange places. Her inner rainbow would help her feel home away from home.

She would soon be needing that inner rainbow in many ways.

Both Stone Castle and Cobblestone Castle were still nervous with anticipation of this possible doom. Communication between the two castles was frequent, but little knowledge of what would transpire was out of their grasps. There were no *givens* to count on. The guessing game was growing weary on them all.

* * *

The midday sun warmed the tanned skin of Shark as he paced the precipice of Stone Castle. His heavy bootsteps seemed to be the only noise around the premises. The scent from the kitchen hearth fire drifted along on what little breeze this summer day had to offer. Hock, the resident chef of the castle, was baking his wondrous breads downstairs away from the other men that seemed bent with the weight of worry over the meteor.

A large black bird glided in and onto the precipice ledge. It skipped over to a small bell along the wall and gently rapped on it with his beak.

The bird's name was Lock, hatched a Tower Raven of Cobblestone Castle. He came from a long lineage of Ravens nurtured for their ability to carry messages over long distances in a short period of time. He was well known in both castles and equally loved. Lock was a favorite to many.

"Hello, Lock!" Shark exclaimed. "You're a sight for sore eyes, my friend. What have you got for us today?"

Lock nodded his head up and down, dancing to and fro chirping, "Lock back! Lock back!" He waited patiently for Shark to rub him on the head and offer up a handful of nuts and berries as payment for his travels. After nibbling on a grape, he raised his leg toward Shark.

Shark gently untied the small piece of parchment attached to the bird's leg. He read it aloud for the bird's benefit, although the Raven would only understand bits and pieces.

Dearest Literati,

We of the castle have noticed a slight change in the color of the meteor star. It appears to be yellowing. Could this be an indication of time frame for us? There is only a slight change in hue, but we ponder its meaning. What are your thoughts on this new development?

Sincerely,
King Marcus

Shark had not noticed any change in coloration of the meteor, despite his hours of staring into the night skies. He stepped inside to share the message with the group.

To his surprise, a number of Literati were already discussing this same topic. It seems that the white star was, in fact, discoloring yellow to some extent. Consulting their literature, it was determined that this occurrence happens as the meteor comes closer. Apparently, the stone was building up heat the closer it came. The book went on to tell that the color would continue to darken into fire red when near to making contact. Unfortunately, there was no timing mentioned in the writing, so this new information was of little value other than solidifying the belief that the meteor had the criteria to create the devastation the Literati feared.

It was confirmed that impact was now not only possible, but likely.

Shark was asked to pen a reply for Lock to deliver back to Cobblestone Castle. He did as he was asked and rubbed Lock on the head and beak. "Big Guy, this isn't good news, buddy. Carry it well. Thank you, Lock."

Though the Tower Ravens knew only a few words and commands, Old Lock had lived long enough to know the sorrow of grave news. He felt this anguish as he took a final glance back toward Shark. With a nod of his head, he dropped off the balcony ledge and flew off into the distance, squawking into the air.

"Lock gone! Lock gone!"

Lilly made good time in her travels. The assent up the Snowy Pass proved more difficult than she'd planned, and the rarely traveled trail was at times hard to follow. As she neared the top of the pass, light snow covered the ground, making travel even more difficult. Still, she pressed on, passing through the main gorge just before nightfall. She began her decent, looking for a suitable location to hole-up for the night.

She was suddenly startled by a rushing bull elk bounding past her in the trail ahead. It seemed odd that an elk would be moving so quickly at dusk. Something seemed out of place, and she quicken her pace, still looking for a proper place to bed down for the night.

Soon she found a small rock ledge just off the trail, and she nestled into it, pulling her cloak up over her head. There was still a light dusting of snow all around her, and she felt uneasy about her cloak being dry of snow and looking out of place in the snowy terrain. Her dark outline was not well disguised.

It was then she heard it. Loud stomping through the brush and bramble of the forest. More importantly, a loud grunt and growl accompanied the heavy footsteps. Something large was tracking the elk, and it was too close for her comfort.

Lilly held her breath, only exhaling into her chest, hoping her breath didn't show on the cold air.

Just as the jostling noise was crossing the trail, it stopped in place. Lilly carefully pulled her cloak open a sliver to try to catch a view of the impending danger.

Then she saw it.

A few strides away from her hiding place stood an enormous Snow Troll, panting and growling.

There are a number of differences between Snow Trolls and their other namesake trolls throughout the forest. Their skin is considerably hairier than the more human-like Cave Trolls. Their hair is a pale gray, almost white. In the early tongues of man, they were called Yautee. Descendants of these trolls were later called Yeti in more modern times.

The troll's nose was pushed up to the air as he turned his head side to side, looking all about him.

Then the beast chuckled.

'Hmmmm," he growled. "I can smell you, but I can't see you. You are no doubt one of those stupid Wild Folk, trespassing over my mountain. Come out, coward!" His wretched voice was frighteningly close as he huffed into the chilly air.

Lilly couldn't breathe and her heart pounded in her chest. *What to do, Lilly, what to do!* Quietly frantic, her mind raced with a way to run, but how? His slow strides still covered far more ground than her limbs could cover. She sat motionless, hoping beyond hope the creature would give up his search for her. Snow Troll eyesight is poor, but their sense of smell is precise.

"Why don't ya come out? Afraid I might boil your bones and gnaw on them?" His voice was as disgusting as anything Lilly had ever heard. It frightened her to the core. Still the Troll sniffed the air. His head turned toward her, and his eyes squinted.

"It seems the Wild Folk are not as apt at hiding as their reputation would elude." The troll's proper verbiage only made his presence that much more frightening. Snow Trolls are inherently smart. Coupled with their brute strength and size, the combination could be deadly.

"I see you've covered your tracks in the snow nicely. You've been taught well, Wild Thing." He began to step in Lilly's direction, still talking, hoping it would keep her still long enough for him to get close.

"Your scent—it's not male. Oh, I smell youth! A young girl, perhaps? Oh, my, my. What ever would bring a young lady of the Wild Folk this far from the pool? Very, very bad for a lass in Snow Troll country, for you are trespassing, and I—I am quite hungry for tender meat!"

Still, the troll could not quite make out Lilly's exact location, but he was sniffing quite close to her now. His head leaned in toward a large pile of leaves, sniffing and squinting his eyes.

"Oh, you are near, young one! I've never tasted female Wild Folk." He was now grunting almost at a whisper as he spoke. "I think ... I think you are about right here..."

The troll's hand extended toward the lump of leaves that was Lilly. Just as his hand was nearing her head, Lilly screamed as loud as she could.

This startled the troll only briefly, but it was enough for Lilly to swing her bamboo staff with all her might. The end of her stick landed squarely on the troll's knee cap, making a shattering, cracking sound liken to a tree limb breaking to fall.

The troll screamed, shocked by the pain and surprise of such a blow.

Lilly bolted down the path as the troll was regaining his senses. With a roar of anger, he lunged in the direction she was running, but his leg collapsed beneath his weight, and he let out a blood-curdling scream that echoed down the path and up against the mountainside.

Still Lilly raced at top speed, not knowing full well the extent of the troll's damage, feeling as if he was dead on her heals about to snatch her up.

On she ran, tears sliding down her face. She had no thoughts to ease her fright. Only RUN.

She ran for what seemed like an hour but was perhaps only thirty minutes. On the downhill slopes, she covered much ground in her frantic race away from the troll. At long last, she collapsed at the edge of a small stream, hoping against hope that there would be no sound of the troll that she was certain was close behind.

But there was no noise. Only near silence filled her ears. On her hands and knees, she wept her hands full, hearing her father's words in her head saying, "Foul things come down from that mountain."

And her father was right. Few Wild Folk had ever lived through an encounter with a Snow Troll. Still, she wept.

And then, very unexpectedly, something happened that soothed her frazzled nerves. There it was. It was that sound. It was the water … the water here in the stream inches from her face. Ever trickling, ever swirling, always soothing to her ears, the water calmed her soul. And yes … there it was—that gentle music. The water harp, somehow strummer her insides with the watery vibrations she had come to love. And there was that other sound, too. It was almost a voice. It was a watery sound that felt like words—liquid lyrics of song that would sooth her.

In that watery sound, she could make out a language of sorts. Real words seemed to come into her. She placed her hands in the stream and kept perfectly still. There it was again. Water lyrics. They called to her.

Press on, little one, for your destiny is beyond this moment. Take rest, young Lilly, for you will need your senses in the days to come.

And with that, the water words stopped. The soothing sounds of the water was still very much engulfing her, but the words had come to pass. She let herself absorb what she'd heard. It was bewildering for her to assess what had just happened. As her mind drifted from the present back to those special moments only seconds ago, she nestled back into the stones near the stream. She pulled her cloak over her head, her mind was overwhelmed, her body exhausted.

She fell into a deep sleep with thoughts of water, trolls, Cobblestone peoples, and even food. She hadn't eaten all day, but food would not be forthcoming until morning.

As her body rested, her dreams were already moving forward on her journey.

Tomorrow, her feet would follow.

* * *

The trickling brook that had lulled Lilly to sleep the night before was now tickling her toes as she stretched her legs from her morning slumber. The opened her eyes fully expecting to see the thatched roof of her home lean-to over her head and to feel the soft woven mat beneath her. She had none of those comforts on this day.

She woke with a start, feeling the aches and pains from her stone bed the night before. She realized where she was. Her head darted back and forth, searching for any sign of the Snow Troll, but to her relief, she was very much alone.

That's when it hit her. She was alone. So very much alone. A pang of fear swept over her as she came to terms with her predicament. There were no comforts of home here. She thought of turning back right here and now, but how? Between here and her home was an angry Snow Troll, and she had no intention of ever finding another one of those petrifying beasts.

"No," she told herself. "My path lies forward to Cobblestone. I must press onward upon my destined path."

It was then that she realized that there was no path here. Somehow, in the darkness of her flight from the troll, she had raced ever farther downhill, abandoning all semblance of trail or path—anything to get away.

No path. Lilly was lost. Again, her heart sank, feeling almost nauseous with the thought of her current conditions. "Here I am, stuck in the woods," she thought. "Now what?"

She tried calming herself by focusing on her destined path. "I'm going to Cobblestone for lessons in life. I will see things I've never seen before. I will meet other folk unlike me. Perk up, Lilly. This is your adventure."

There she sat, battling wits with her inner self. She also determined that she was famished. Her stomach growled beneath her woven cloak. She remembered her batch of snails in her pouch. She quickly dug them out and placed the bag in the creek before her, hoping to revive them enough to complete her journey and use them as barter for whatever she would need when she arrived.

Still, her stomach growled.

Although the summer morning was quite warm, the morning dew had chilled her. She pulled open another of her pouches and retrieved her fire starter kit. It consisted of a small stick bow and a string. She also scratched around the ground nearby and found some dry cedar and pine needles, which she scooped into a pile atop a flat rock near the stream. She wound a dry stick into the bow and string and began spinning it, building friction within the dry needles. Soon, a puff of smoke emerged and then a flame came through. She quickly piled a few leaves and small sticks on top, increasing the flames. She pulled two large snails from her pouch in the creek and tossed them into the fire to cook. Soon the crackle snap of the shells popping could be heard. She pushed the snails out of the fire to cool and warmed her damp hands around the fire.

She pried open the snails and ate her small morning breakfast. She desperately wanted to eat more but chose to keep back as many snails as possible for barter.

Now, she faced her predicament. She was lost.

She then remembered the map given to her by her father. She pulled if from a pouch and unrolled it into her lap. As her father warned her, she could not read the penned words, but she hoped that the pictures would be helpful in determining her whereabouts.

What little she knew about maps told her that the top of all maps is North. Looking eastward toward the rising sun, she quickly spun the map to match the east on the map with the sunrise.

"Poppa said to go south and cross the river, then veer west." In staring at the map, she saw her original path, the river, as well as other points of interest. South was not a problem. She understood the path of the sun as a reference, but she had no idea if she was east or west of the southerly trail. She eventually surmised that if she was west of the trail going south, she would find the westward trail after crossing the river somewhere ahead of her. But if she was east of the path, she would miss it altogether.

She stared down at the map in her hands. If she was east of the southward trail and she never found the westward trail, her travel would eventually lead her to another trail that was drawn much larger on the map. Its line was drawn thicker and more prominent on the map. *Perhaps that trail is actually the Old Road?* She had heard the old tales told around her home about the Old Road that connected Cobblestone to Stone Castle and then beyond to the far north to Troll Country and the Dark Lands. As a last resort, if she missed the westward trail completely, she could at least go west on the Old Road and find Cobblestone. So, given this revelation, she donned her things to go south.

This information comforted her. She doused her fire and sat back to take in her surroundings. Something about the nature around her seemed far more intense than that of home. Perhaps it was the lack of others nearby that intensified her senses. Maybe it was just a special morning on her new journey. No matter! These stirrings filled her heart and her "Inner Rainbow." The trickling of the brook echoed louder in her ears than ever before. The chirping of the birds was more crisp than usual. Even the barking of the squirrels seemed comical and playful. A sense of joy lightened her step. *How wonderful*, she thought.

As she stepped across the brook, she was elated to see a large river clam just beneath the surface. She snatched it up and tucked it away in her pouch. She soon found another, then another. She sauntered down the brook for a bit, pulling still more clams from the water. These would make great barter for her journey! She had hoped that following the brook would perhaps run her into the trail she'd lost. Alas, no. She turned her attention from the creekside and made her way south.

A few hours later, she found herself in the midst of a large batch of beautiful mushrooms. She had always been a student of mushroom hunting, knowing all the edible varieties by heart. "Don't pick the yellow toadstools with the red dots!" her father would always remind her. "They're bloody bad for ya! Poison!"

She pondered why anyone in the world would bother to pick those nasty little mushrooms.

She steered clear of the bad mushrooms and filled her pouch with a nice stash of delicate ones and even some dead-bark fins, which are a very hearty and thick fungus that was a mainstay for her people of the village. Roasted over flame, they were not only delicious, but also contained many nutrients healthy for the body. It was a great find for her, helping her stockpile her supplies for both travel and future bartering.

As the midday sun heated the forest, Lilly traversed the rough terrain, crossing hills and rocky foothills and briar patches in her southward travel. The sharp thorns not only tore at her skin, but also burned and itched profusely afterward. She longed for another creek or brook to rinse her skin free of the briar poisons, but her way led only upward away from water. She was beginning to get quite thirsty, too. She had no way of carrying water and her thirst was weighing her down to some degree.

But Lilly was not worried about finding water. She knew her inner rainbow and the water's tune would lead her to it.

Those voices she could always count on. They would be essential on this trek … in ways she could never imagine.

The lower halls of Cobblestone Castle were being stockpiled with all sorts of non-perishable goods. Large barrel casks were filled with fresh water should the city's water source be contaminated. Salted meats were hung high in the rafters, safe from any rising water. Apples and pears were in bushel baskets, and even satchels of Mallow Leaf tobacco were settled into the high shelves along the walls. Woven blankets were kept dry in separate rooms in case fire set them ablaze, jeopardizing the rest of the hoard of supplies.

Lock, the Tower Raven, had delivered the news of what was already suspected. The meteor was indeed heating up for impact. The unease in the air was becoming noticeable by some of the townsfolk. The strange comings and goings to and from the castle gave way to some suspicion throughout the city. *Just what's going on at the capital?*

* * *

Meanwhile, the council hall of Stone Castle was experiencing turmoil as well.

Elias addressed the murmuring crowd. "Brothers, I understand your concerns. We are in this together. The coloring of the meteor proves its coming. We still have no time frame for impact. Our gatherers have filled our stores with food and weaponry. We are doing what we can."

Young Daniel was frustrated with the lack of forward motion, hoping more could be done. To him, they were all treading water, and the impatience of youth was wearing thin. Uncharacteristically, he spoke out of turn. "Elias! What word from Tolk?"

Elias was gritting his teeth. "Young Squire Daniel, need I remind you of your status as squire?" His words punched at Daniel like a fist. "Tolk will speak when he is ready, and ONLY when he is ready. The simplicity of youth is clouding your impatience. I implore you to stifle your mouth before I forever shut it! You would do well to hide your pompous self until called for ... should I EVER do so again! Tolk has forgotten more than you will ever learn, and you had best recognize that with utter respect and diligence toward him!"

Daniel humbly apologized, but deep in his heart, he was frustrated and angered that more could not be done. In his humble opinion, the Great Literati were not living up to their name. He also realized that the rest of this crowd harboured the same thoughts that only he was willing to state. But, he paid dearly for his utterings, and that would stand a very long time amid such company. Right or wrong, he'd made his ill-received point.

Still the crowd mumbled. Little more was settled, much to Daniel's dismay.

Meanwhile, well above the council hall in the high tower of the eldest elder, Tolk was scribing as fast as his arthritic hands could push quill and ink onto parchment. Some of his writings were of his usual eloquent rhythmic and rhyming prose of prophesy. Others were elaborate drawings of fire and stone, almost climbing from the pages of his laborious work. He hadn't eaten in three days. The other Literati had left food and gallons of water for him at the door, but water was his only mainstay in his current state of mind. Sweat dripped from his brow, mixing with the inks and scratches on the parchment beneath his weary head. His energy was waning. His body was failing. Only his brilliant mind was sustaining him through this, his final and most important work.

Tolk was dying … lingering long enough to pen words that would be studied for generations to come. He operated under both fear and desperation, pressing forward with the fortitude and fervency that perhaps only a dying man could muster. In his mind, he raced the death clock-watch against the imperative prophesy he deemed paramount. As his body faltered, his mind soared to new heights. This story was unfolding before his very eyes as he saw bits and pieces of the future blinking through his head. *I simply MUST get this penned …*

… even if it kills me.

Sadly, it would.

Lilly's journey southward did not reveal the westward trail that she'd hoped she'd find. Per her previous determination, she continued southward in hopes of finding the next big trail that might be The Old Road.

Her path was a treacherous hike. The mapped trails were trails because of their ease of travel. Simply traveling south did not offer a simplistic avenue through the rough countryside. Cliffs opened to sheer ledges, and where the route flattened, the briars took over, again tearing at skin and psyche. Rock bruises and briar lacerations marred her skin, and her thirst cracked her lips and blurred her eyes. Her hair stuck to the back of her neck, sweat gluing dirt and grime into places she didn't know she had. She itched. Her eyes burned. Her muscles ached. Still her determination did not falter. Judging distances by her father's map, she was certain she was nearing the big path of The Old Road.

She finally crested a steep hill and peered over the top. She hoped she would finally catch a glimpse of something resembling a path. What she found was much better.

The Old Road paralleled the bluff known as Bad Fall. The fearsome bluff Lilly had just ascended meandered for miles, bending and turning its jagged edges, making travel northward barely passable other than the long perimeter path of the Old Road. Lilly had just climbed this chasm from the north going south. She had surprisingly eluded the "Bad Fall" for which this bluff was aptly named. She knew nothing of its foreboding name but felt the rigors of having climbed it. Also, to her fortune, just across the Old Road was a spring trickling from out of the rock bluff wall. She mashed her face against the cold stone, sucking up water and rinsing her body with the refreshing water. It was an oasis to her.

The road near her feet simply must be The Old Road, she surmised. It had been heavily traveled, although there were no travelers this late evening.

The sun was falling in the westward sky, and Lilly was certain that her travels had led her—at the very least, in a positive direction for her destination. *This MUST be the old road.*

"I need only travel west now." She was right, but her body had endured all it could for one day. She needed rest badly, and it seemed apparent that there were enough hiding places nearby that she could rest herself and bed down just out of view and refresh herself yet again in the spring water in the morn. She would man-up and start the day anew. Tomorrow was a new day, and this little foreign girl was overdue for a good night's sleep. Her body still ached from the night before, but her mind raced with wondrous thoughts of being that much nearer to her journey's pinnacle. She was almost to Cobblestone. And oh, the glory!

* * *

Lilly had tucked herself beneath the rock ledge of the bluff near the spring. Her woven cloak made her nearly disappear into a pile along the bluff's edge. She had settled into a deep sleep and had rested from nightfall until morning. The warm sun had already risen when she awakened.

With a stretch and a yawn, she meandered back to the spring and took a long drink of water. It was cool upon her dry lips, and it revived her for her new day. Cobblestone awaited her, and she was excited to be on her way. She set her sights westward and walked along the Old Road almost skipping as she traveled.

After a couple hours of travel, she was surprised to hear the sound of galloping hooves ahead. A dark horse and a lone rider appeared in a cloud of dust, slowing to a stop as he came near. His demeanor was dry, and his body language was not pleasant. Lilly could feel his glare peering into her. He sized up this young lady dressed in leaves and pondered his next moves. His gruff voice was eerie, and the scowl he wore set Lilly on the alert. This was not a nice person, and his speech was about to prove it.

"Hello there, young lady. Aren't you a pretty thing, for a Wild Folk. You look like you could use a companion. I can help you out with that, you know." The rider dismantled his horse and stepping close to Lilly, eyeing her top to bottom.

"What ya got in them pouches there, Lassy? Let's take a look, shall we?"

The man reached his hand toward Lilly's pouch, but she stepped back and warned him.

"Keep back! I don't want any trouble! Go on about your business." Lilly was frightened of the man but tried to present herself as strong and confident. This guy was trouble, and she knew it. Maybe her mother was right about these Cobblestone people being unpleasant and rude. She warned him once more.

"Stay back! I mean business!"

The man's nasty grin showed that he had no intention of backing off. He planned to have his way with her after stealing what little she might have in her pouches. Again, he stepped toward her, almost pawing at her.

Just as his hand grabbed her arm, Lilly reacted out of instinct. Her father's lessons were etched deeply in her mind. She spun her bamboo stick breaking his forearm. Another roundhouse swing cracked him on the back of the skull, sending him to the ground in a slumped pile, grasping his broken arm in a rage. Dazed and furious he lunged once more toward Lilly, trying to tug on her cloak, but it was to no avail. One more swift crack of her stick had the man knocked unconscious, bleeding from his brow.

Lilly didn't know what to do next. A nearly lifeless man lay at her feet, and his horse simply stared at her not knowing his next moves either. She didn't know how to ride a horse and didn't want to steal it anyway. She finally gave in and elected to walk on leaving the thug roadside behind her. When he came to, she'd be well ahead of him toward Cobblestone. If she hadn't knocked all of the sense out of him, he would continue on nursing his wounds. If he elected to chase after her, she would hear him coming and hide until he passed. Either way, she marched on, hoping that the next person she encountered would be far more pleasant than the last.

Before she turned to leave, she gave the man's horse a swift smack on the rear, and the horse bolted away at top speed.

"That should teach him a lesson! Do good, or don't do—just like Momma always said."

A small piece of her felt triumphant in her leveling of an aggressor. Terrifying as it was, it proved to be a confidence builder. She had held her own in the face of imminent danger. She saved herself and eliminated the threat of harm in seconds. Her father had taught her well, and it proved valuable with her very first encounter with a stranger. Surely, all of Cobblestone would not be such ruffians. Her mother's words still lingered in her mind, and she hoped against hope that Mom's assessment would not be accurate overall. *This was a rare encounter*, she told herself. *Cobblestone will be welcoming.*

So, she pressed on westward, still somehow looking forward to her next encounters. She teased herself thinking about how hungry she was and that maybe pig and cow would be a welcome meal. *I think I could eat the hooves about now!*

Another hour of travel had the midday sun warming her face. The Old Road was quiet this day, and her travel was a pleasant walk. She rounded the next corner of the road and the terrain opened before her. There it was! Cobblestone! Rooftops could be seen in the distance, and the peak of the tower of the castle glistened blue in the sunlight. The houses spanned the valley before her and spread up onto the hillside closer to the castle. Thatched roofs and rock buildings filled the landscape before her. Small shanty barns were full of hay, and wagon carts of other goods were tucked alongside wooden shelters. Fenced animals could be seen on grassy hillsides. It was, perhaps, the most beautiful sight she'd ever seen. She had found Cobblestone, and her heart raced with the sight of it all!

How could they build so many buildings and towers and fences?!?!

The girl was city-struck, and she was feeling every tingle of emotion that accompanied it. The thatched hutches and pretty gardens of her home were equally beautiful in many ways, but the sheer grandeur of these sights and sounds was no match for home.

Soon, as she walked, other travelers appeared on the road. A man and women were walking a small heard of goats out of town. Their children followed, tossing stones from the path, playfully doing what little kids do. It seemed so quaint to Lilly, a family on a journey together. She said *hello* and kept on walking, taking in all her surroundings. She didn't notice the strange glances the couple exchanged after she was gone. The girl *did* look out of place, even in a city full of different varieties of people. It didn't seem to bother the couple. They just shrugged their shoulders and continued on their way.

She felt a little awkward, dressed in only her woven cloak, but most of the people gave little notice.

Soon, she met still more travelers on the road. She made small talk with several, feeling as if she was engulfed in real civilization for the first time. The hustle, the bustle, the children scampering through the streets, it was all beautiful to her. Flower boxes in the windowsills overflowed with color. Peddlers were selling shoes and special spices from horse-drawn carts. Vegetables were growing in nearly every yard. The sights and smells overwhelmed her.

As she entered the city, she settled into a small bench, simply taking in everything she could. At that moment, her mind drifted back to a particular moment from her youth. It was a moment she shared with her grandfather. Her grandfather was a stronghold for her when she was young. He often said many things that didn't quite register with her young mind. He reached her in many ways, but one particular topic came back to her in this moment. With new sights and sounds filling her mind, one thought reentered her brain. It was a saying she did not understand at the time of her early youth, but now those words hit home with her. The words her grandfather had spoken years ago when she was a wee lass of ten now echoed in her head.

As the sights, smells and sounds engulfed her, her grandfather's words seemed to embrace her.

"Remember, Miss Lilly, to always FEEL."

Her youthful mind questioned him. "I don't understand, Grand-Poppa?"

"In this life," he quoted, "You will endure great sorrow, great joy—so very much life thrown at you. All I ask is that you FEEL it."

Lilly wasn't certain of what the old man was trying to show her. She finally asked him, "Why would I want to feel sorrow?"

The old man smiled in his response. "Feeling is the only way that you will know that you are alive. Don't push life aside. Embrace it."

At this very moment, in this new place—only now did she fully understand what her grandfather had told her so many years ago.

Quietly she whispered to herself. "Today I FEEL, Grand-Poppa. I FEEL!"

* * *

Lilly found a small brook on the edge of town and stopped for a drink. She splashed the back of her neck to cool her down and rinsed her hands.

"Where do I go first?" she asked herself.

A passerby stopped as she passed. She gave Lilly an inquisitive glance. "You look different," she said. "Your first time to Cobblestone?"

Lilly was surprised at her pleasant tone. She hadn't witnessed much cordial behavior up to this point. She was happy to answer. "Yes! Your city is quite beautiful!"

The young lady was surprised to hear such eloquent language from Lilly. Given her appearance, it was hard to judge her character. With a smile, the lady continued, "Yes, it is. I love it here. The autumn is especially pretty when the trees change. Will you be staying that long?"

Lilly was perplexed with the lady's question. She hadn't really pondered staying longer than she had told her father. The fall color would be a sight to behold. "No," Lilly replied, sounding a bit downhearted. "I'd dearly love to see it. I bet it's breathtaking."

"Shame," the woman replied. "Cobblestone has its faults, but I wouldn't want to live anywhere else. They call me Jen. Perhaps we will cross paths again during your stay."

"I should hope so!" Lilly replied. "I could use a guide! I am Lilly."

We will see what we can do about that," Jen commented. "I'm quite busy the next few days, but I'm sure I'll see you around. I will try to help. For now, I strongly suggest seeing Margarite at The Wayfarer. It's an Inn about five blocks ahead. She's hard to get to know, but she's awesome. She took me in when I first arrived."

"Arrived? From where did you come? You seem … um … local."

Jen chuckled. "Then perhaps I've been here long enough for Cobblestone to rub off!"

The two chatted for a short while longer, and Jen needed to move along about her business. As she turned to leave, she reminded Lilly of her suggestion. "See Margarite."

Lilly agreed and continued walking into the city. It seemed her every sense was overflowing. Everything pleased her. Aside from the visual beauty, the sounds of feet and hooves on the cobblestone streets was almost music to her ears. The smells were fantastic. She knew the scent of cooked meat from her own village. On rare occasions, her people would cook rabbit or squirrel over the fire in the winter months when vegetables were in short supply. But there was something else she smelled. She couldn't recognize or imagine what type of food it could be, but its sweet aroma was simply wonderful. Her stomach was growling aloud, and she was quite ready to fill it with something new and exciting.

Before she knew it, she stood before the steps of The Wayfarer Inn and Tavern. It was a large stone building with a tile roof and open windows. The smell she was seeking was flowing out around the colorful curtains and out into the streets. Intimidating as it was, Lilly began the flight of steps to the door.

Before she could reach the top, she was startled by the door swinging open and the figure of an older lady dressed in the biggest dark red dress Lilly had ever seen. The lady's damp apron appeared as if it could have been white at some point, but clearly was discolored with a dusty brown hue all about. The figure stopped mid-step and eyed down at Lilly.

"There will be no beggars here, young lady!" the woman snapped. "Be gone on down the road with ya."

Lilly was angered by the blunt comment but held her temper and spoke up. "I'm no beggar!"

The woman's brow furrowed. "Then what are ya, then, Lassy?"

"I'm from the Iceland River Pool," Lilly exclaimed. "I should like to sample your foods that smell so lovely."

The woman still held a gruff stare. She was silent for what seemed an eternity to Lilly. She finally broke her silence with a grunt. "Humph. Got money, do ya, Lassy?"

"No ma'am, but I have goods to barter."

The woman never let up her frown. "Goods, huh? What would a bag of trash like you have to barter with me?"

Lilly was furious. She stopped her way further up the steps. "I'm no bag of trash, either, you wicked woman!"

The lady was taken aback with the girl's fortitude and fiery nature. "Excuse me, Lassy! I thought someone had dumped a bail of hay on me doorstep, I did!"

Lilly's blood was boiling. "Just because I don't dress like you uppity folk doesn't mean I'm not civilized and worthy of respect!"

The woman still stared, pondering her next moves. Her head tilted. "Hummm. You're one of them Wild Folk, aren't ya, Lassy?"

"ERRRR!" growled Lilly. "We are NOT WILD! We are just folk and that's that!"

"Humph," the woman grunted again, letting a bit of smile escape her scowl. "Ya got spunk, Lassy, I'll give ya that. You seemed to have the purdy words even if yer clothes are lookin' like the bottom of the barn stall."

Lilly would have been beyond mad if it weren't for the slight smile she was bending from the woman. She was making at least a little progress. This time she attempted to smile as well. "We don't dress like you Cobblers, but we are very much civilized!"

"Cobblers? We only have one in town, and he fixes boots down by Smitty's well."

"Are you going to barter with me, or shall I take my special wares to some other insulting abode?"

The woman chuckled out loud. "You sure do have them fancy words, young-un. Just what ya got in them pouches?"

Lilly was glad to have finally broken the ice between them. "I have fresh yellow mushrooms and some black bark mushrooms, too … from the Deep Forest! I also have the biggest and finest snails fresh from the Iceland Pool. Alive still!"

"Well, now, do ya, Lassy?"

Lilly pulled a small handful of mushrooms from her pouch to show.

"Them's mighty nice ones! How about them snails yer so proud of?"

Lilly pulled two glorious snails out into view, their green and brown hues shining in the evening sunset.

"Well, now," the lady said again. "Them's the biggest I've ever seen! A hungry sailor would pay a mighty shilling for a half dozen of those purdies!"

"I'd trade a half dozen of those for a hot meal. I'm not used to hot meals."

The lady raised an eyebrow. "Really, Lassy? I grill the best steak in all of Cobblestone!"

Lilly's eyes lit up. "Oh, wonderful! Is that pig and cow?"

The lady was dumbfounded. "Lordy, Lassy, yer a fine piece of work, ya are. It's, humph, cow, if you must. But listen, now, girly, you'll have to pull off that rat's nest of a cloak before you enter my Inn."

Lilly quickly began pulling off her cloak.

"OH, MY BLAZES, LASSY! YER BUCK NAKED! Put it back on, back on quickly afore somebody's a seein' ya!"

Lilly was confused. Nakedness was quite common in her village. No one thought anything of it. Their cloaks were for warmth or hiding.

"Well, which is it, ma'am?" Lilly only smiled.

"Yer full of surprises, girly. Why, I never …" her voice trailed off. "Wait here. I'll be right back. And don't be touchin' nothin' with them grimy paws."

Something told Lilly that she must have now met Margarite, just as Jen had mentioned. She was indeed a little difficult to get to know, but she was certain meeting her was the right thing for her to do. Plus! She was getting a hot new meal of some sort. She was so excited.

Shortly, Margarite emerged with a large yellow bath robe. Quickly, Lassy, put this on and leave that bear-skin rug of yers behind the barrels over there. No one in their right mind would take it!"

Lilly frowned on that last comment a little, but let it slide. She'd worked for three days weaving her cloak. It was quite something back home. But alas, she was not home, and it suited her just fine to be mingling with these new people. In fact, she was elated and could not wait for her eating experience.

Margarite led her to a dark corner table in the back of the seating area. "I'll be back in a jiffy," she stated.

It wasn't long until Margarite returned with a platter full of unrecognizable food for Lilly. Lilly looked surprised, but graciously thanked her. "So, you fire it?" she asked.

"Fire it?" Both now looked confused.

"Oh, I'm sorry, Margarite. That's what we call it. Burn it a little."

"I didn't burn nothin', Lassy! You eat that and try not to eat the plate! And how did you know my name, anyway?"

Lilly smiled. "Call it a hunch."

Margarite huffed away and left Lilly to her steak, potato and a small round and brown rock-looking thing that was completely foreign to Lilly. She elected to start with the cow. It was hot to the touch as she picked it up with both hands and tasted. It was very different than her expectations, but she was quite happy. She was so very hungry, that it didn't matter how different it was. The potato was good, too, but she'd have preferred it raw.

She then picked up the brown rock thing and sniffed. Oh, it was that wonderful smell from outside! "What is this stuff?" she asked herself. She took a large bite out of the golden yeast roll. Her eyes widened, and she crammed the rest of the entire roll into her mouth, almost crying with emotion.

She chewed and chewed, not wanting to swallow just yet … savoring every ounce. "Wow!" she mumbled through her mouthful of bread. "This stuff is worth fighting a troll for!"

"Margarite!" she yelled. "More rocks!"

10

Miles from Cobblestone, Tolk sat gazing at the piles of parchment neatly stacked all around him. All were labeled and set in order. Countless crudely-scratched drawings and runes filled the pages alongside untold writings of prophesy eerily penned in rhyme and rhythm. His aged hands had stopped writing. His trance-like state was fading. He was coming-to with only a few precise thoughts forming in his mind. His stiff body eased up from his desk, and his ancient legs inched toward the door. A burning desire welled up within him giving him energy where there was none. Through sheer determination only he pushed forward as fast as he could muster. He must see the Literati.

Tolk had somehow managed the descent of the staircase and followed his ears to the sounds of voices in the council hall. Dead silence ensued as he drug himself through the open door. Many gasped at the sight of this poor decrepit man trembling before them. His face had an urgency none in this room had ever seen on his face before. Tolk tried to shout, but his voice could only deliver a loud whisper. In the silence of the room, that dry whisper was heard by all.

Tolk shouted his whisper.

"Worry not of the comet! Nurture the Myrtos! Split the shard ..."

As his voice trailed off, Tolk's body collapsed to the floor, falling limp with a thud. The Literati raced to his side whisking his body onto a nearby cot. Elias held the man's head in his hands, pleading for him to answer.

"Tolk! Tolk, stay with us!"

It was of little use. Tolk had spent every ounce of energy left within his body. The old man shakily again whispered the last three words he would ever speak.

"Nurture the Myrtos ..."

With that, Tolk's eyes closed. His breathing stopped. His pulse slipped away. His face grew pale.

Amid the sorrow, tears, and confusion, alongside men who loved him dearly, Tolk—the oldest and wisest of Literati ever born ... died.

11

The banks of the Iceland Pool had changed little since Lilly's departure. The gardens were still cared for, the fire pits cleaned, snails were still being plucked from the waterline. Despite the commonplace occurrences going on, Lilly's village was missing her playful spirit. Her mother grew withdrawn, often staring up at the trail that Lilly hiked on her ascent toward Cobblestone. Each day she prayed Lilly's face would crest the mountain and appear through the trees, sporting her playful grin for which she was so well-known. The incessant questions from Lilly to her mother were sometimes considered annoying but were now sorely missed. All worried for her wellbeing.

"Momma," called Kato. "When's Lee-Lee coming home?"

It was a question Lilly's mother tried to answer numerous times daily. She'd been asking herself that same question, knowing full well that it would not be for many more days. The new moon was weeks away, and it ate at her heart constantly.

Kato's father overheard him and placed him on his lap, comforting him in a hug. "Son, she will be back the same way she left ... when she's good and ready. She promised she'd return by the next moon. That's a way off, I'm afraid. Until then, let's keep busy and not think about it."

But in his heart, he knew that was a lie. He'd be thinking about her every moment until she hugged him again.

12

Lilly could not have picked a better place to land in Cobblestone. Despite her gruff exterior, Margarite was a softy at heart. She given Lilly a room for a few nights, making the agreement that Lilly would do dishes in the evening and mop floors to earn her keep. Mopping was quite foreign to Lilly, given that she'd never set foot on a floor until she'd walked into the Wayfarer Inn. Thanks to Jen's advice, she was set up nicely for her stay in the big city.

Margarite allowed Lilly to bundle up her cloak and bring it inside, provided she set it outside her bedroom window on the roof. She had mumbled something about bugs and stench as she'd walked away, but Lilly only smiled, knowing she was in good hands in this cozy and safe spot.

She reflected on her first "city folk" meal a few hours earlier. She had complimented Margarite on her cow, which really wasn't a lie. It wasn't half bad. It was just quite different than anything she'd ever tried. The yeast rolls were another thing altogether. She had devoured five as fast as Margarite could bring them. She had raved over them, telling

Margarite that they were simply the best thing she'd ever eaten, period. That was before Margarite suggested she try the golden slippery stuff on the side plate as a topping for her rolls. She did as she was told, pasting a pile of butter on top. It was, to Lilly, as if the Gods had rained down the nectars of Heaven right onto her plate.

"Where does this come from?!" Lilly exclaimed.

"Comes from my kitchen, Lassy, and yer making quite the hog out of yourself."

"It's more than wonderful! What do you call it?"

"Has many names, girl. Bread. Rolls. You can slice it and heat it again and call it toast."

Lilly was bewildered. "You MUST show me where to pick it!"

Margarite shook her head. "Lassy, another day. You're exhausting me."

So, Lilly was over-full and staring out the window of her room, pondering her unbelievable day. Margarite had sent a bowl of hot water to her room for her to bathe. This, too, was a special moment for her. She'd never bathed in anything but the Iceland Pool, which was quite cool, even in summer. This hot water was amazing. It seemed as if her sore muscles and scrapes from her travels rinsed away. She felt and was cleaner than she'd ever been. She felt as if she could fall asleep standing up at the window.

Margarite had showed her the bed, but she'd simply gazed at it, not knowing fully what had been suggested. "Pull back the covers, Lassy, and jump yer body in and nestle up! I keep the best feather-ticks in town. You should be comfy."

Lilly found most of Margarite's descriptions of all the foreign things to be vague at best, but so far, she loved each and every suggestion the old woman had for her. She felt pampered in this very basic pauper's room—lost in a magical world of comfort. Simple as these things were, they were all beyond her wildest imagination. *Wait 'til Momma and Poppa hear about this!*

She felt a pang guilt as thoughts of her family came to mind. Leaving them was perhaps the hardest thing she'd ever done. She found herself missing them all, even in this wonderland of a city. Her mind and belly were fuller than they'd ever been. It was both strange and wonderful to her.

She continued to gaze out her room's window. The night sky was full of stars and a hint of Cobblestone Castle could be seen on the horizon. It was so beautiful to her. Rooftop after rooftop extended before her. Windows with candles sparkled like the fireflies back home. It was almost too much. Such wonder. Such different lives.

She then noticed something that seemed peculiar to her. Many of the townsfolk had climbed out of their windows and were sitting on the rooftops enjoying the night air. Lilly could not resist. Her window eased open, and she slid out onto the roof. The night sky seemed to engulf her. She wondered if her special star would shine here like it did back home. She had lovingly named it Kato, after her little brother. She felt they both shined. Maybe it would shine for her here.

As she suspected, her personal star sparkled among the rest, only something was different. It looked yellow here in the city. Maybe it was reflecting something from here. Fires, maybe? Sure enough, it was yellow, but that didn't hamper Lilly's joyous mood. She sat and gazed for a few minutes but felt sleep coming on fast.

Lilly climbed back into her room and disrobed. She wasn't sure if one "went to bed" with clothing on or not. It seemed right to her or perhaps more home-like to be shed of clothing. Those blankets would keep her warm like the woven kind she was familiar with.

She pulled back the quilt from the surface of the bed and did her best to follow Margarite's instructions of jumping herself in. With a pounce, she landed as if she was swimming back home. To her surprise, she melted into the softest pile of cushioned comfort she'd ever felt. This would be like sleeping in the clouds, she thought.

She edged the quilt up to her neck and nestled in. “This is heavenly,” she whispered to herself. “What in the world will tomorrow show me?”

With wondrous thoughts and memories of today flowing through her head, Lilly drifted off into the deepest and best sleep ever. She dozed off in seconds, smiling ear to ear in her sleep.

Lilly had found Utopia.

13

The ringing sound of the raven bell could be heard in the upper tower of Cobblestone Castle. The graying black feather of Lock rapped on the bell string and awaited his head rub and handful of nuts and berries.

The king was given this note:

Dearest King Marcus,

I regret to inform you that our elder, Tolk has passed. He has penned much in regard to the meteor. We are studying and will inform soon. For now, we mourn.

Elias

"Hummm," the king grunted. "So, Tolk is dead. Pity. He was a wealth of knowledge for us. Let's hope the rest of our intelligent puppets there can decipher his writings."

"Well," said Byron, the king's closest advisor, "that'll slow things down for certain."

"Nonsense. We've gotten emergency supplies stock piled and we have our next mission lying in wait."

Byron looked worried. "If we live."

The king raised a knowing eyebrow. "Yes, if we live…"

At that moment, another tower raven landed on the castle precipice. Both men were startled by the motion and wondered why another bird would have been sent so soon. Byron quickly untied the parchment from the bird's leg and handed it to the king.

As the king read through the words within, his eyes squinted with the look of both confusion and satisfaction.

Byron stood patiently for as long as he could stand. "Sire, what is it?"

"Byron, my friend. It's Tolk's last words."

"What do you make of them?"

"It's all gibberish except for the best part. That's all we care!" The king wore a sly grin.

"Well?" asked Byron. "TELL! What is it?"

"He says, 'Worry not about the meteor'!"

14

The sun had already risen when Lilly's eyes opened. It startled her awake. It was rare that anyone in her pod slept until sunup. For a brief moment she was disoriented in her surroundings, but the events of yesterday flooded back instantly. She eased back into her covers and relished the moment. She wondered if all of Cobblestone had such rich quarters in which to live. Was she being treated like royalty? The absolute comfort of this place was wonderful for her.

She peered down to the foot of the bed. Her two changes of clothing were folded neatly waiting for her. She secretly wanted to wear the fuzzy robe Margarite had given her last evening. It was soft to the touch, much more so than her woven cloak. She eventually decided to try on one of the outfits so she could start her day. She was anxious to get moving. She couldn't wait to see more of what the city had to offer.

She settled on the first of the two parcels of clothing Margarite had given her. It was a simple red and white checkered dress with slight frills on the sleeves. She slid it over her body and looked herself over.

Strangely, she still felt naked, which suited her fine. It was a more natural feel to her than the heavy robe she wore last night.

"I certainly couldn't hide wearing this thing!" she said out loud. "I guess I'll trust Margarite. She's been wonderful so far."

She slid on a pair of slipper-shoes that reminded her of her sandals, only much softer. They felt nice wrapping her feet.

She went downstairs and found Margarite waiting on tables of seafaring men, bringing food and drink to them all, talking up a storm with each of them. She saw Lilly enter and quickly led her aside.

"Don't be lingerin' here long, Lassy. These men get ideas."

As usual, Lilly looked blank but took Margarite's words to heart.

"Now, Lassy, I know you are on some sort of holiday, but don't be forgettin' ya got chores this evenin'. Back here before dark, ya hearin' me?"

"Yes, ma'am," Lilly chirped. "I'll be back."

"Not yet, Lassy." Margarite slid two large biscuits from a table nearby and handed them to Lilly. "Ya need to eat a little somethin', girl."

Lilly gladly accepted and stepped away and out the front door. Margarite had given her some money for her remaining mushrooms and snails she'd brought for barter. Lilly had no idea what each coin was worth, but she let them jingle in her front pocket for her trip through town.

She plopped down on the front steps, taking in the smells of town. She took her first bite of biscuit and quickly crammed the rest into her mouth. This bread stuff was worth every step of her journey.

As she stepped into the cobblestone street outside the Inn, she was amazed to see cultivated flowers in wooden containers outside the shutters of the windows. She had just learned the terms shutter and window last night from Margarite along with a hundred other words she was trying to remember. In her village, flowers grew where they would, and they were left there to enjoy. Planting was for fruits and vegetables, and those were tucked away out of view in a more natural way. Pretty as these were, it seemed like a waste of time.

Suddenly, Lilly was startled and scared. Ahead of her in the road was a wolf walking right toward her! She quickly tucked out of view beside a rock pillar of one of the buildings. She eased her head around the corner just enough to watch the beast.

Again, she was amazed. The townspeople paid little or no attention to this fierce, wild animal. It was walking right near them! Soon, the animal turned its attention to a man selling wares from a wooden cart. The man smiled and pulled a piece of dried meat from his pocket and walked over to it. The dog sat patiently and wagged its tail, and the man rubbed its ears and fed it the meat.

"Lordy! I thought surely he'd lose his arm!"

Soon the dog continued down the street toward her location. Lilly stood stone still hoping the dog would walk on by. But as the dog neared, it pushed its nose into the air and sniffed. The dog turned, looked right at her, then walked on over.

Lilly stood paralyzed, trying not to breathe. She had her eyes closed, and she trembled down her spine. The dog sauntered up to her and sniffed her dress. She let out a little squeak, but it didn't phase the dog at all. He sat down and wagged his tail.

Lilly slowly opened her eyes. There the beast was. Reminding herself of how the man had treated the dog, she did her best to do the same. She delicately reached her fist over the dog's head. It pushed its nose up to smell her, and she recoiled. Slowly, she did the same, this time facing her fear. Her fist unclenched, and she again reached over his head, this time her hand nestling into the dog's soft fur. It was quite the sensation for her feeling such fur and the warmth of his body.

Perhaps out of instinct, Lilly found herself speaking to the dog.

"You're beautiful, but I don't have any food for you."

The dog exhaled as if to say, "Well, shoot." It turned away and walked on down the street.

"Wow," she thought. "I just laid hands on a wolf and lived!"

Most of the rest of her day was uneventful, but every single small thing she encountered filled her with awe. There was so much to see and touch.

There were a couple of things she noticed that really struck a chord in her. Later in the day, she witnessed two men fighting outside a tavern. People did not fight with fists in her village. Angered people would challenge one another with bamboo. At the end of the day, no one was truly injured, and the fight was settled. In this instance, blood poured from each man. It seemed barbaric to her—uncivilized even, and it felt out of place in this pristine village.

Another oddity that was remarkable to her was how the city drained water from the rains. There were rock ditches and pathways to direct water away from the buildings, always running downhill out of sight. Her village never needed such an arrangement. These people thought of everything down to storm drain grates in the street. It was a fascinating concept.

She visited with a few people along the way, asking more questions than they more were willing to answer. Still, it was educational and fun for her. She bought a piece of food that was made of some sort of bread, but it had a delicious filling of berry soup. For her, it was one more wonderful way to eat bread. The man called it pie, and when she gave him one of her coins, he gave her four back. That was confusing, but the man had a face she trusted, and she merely acted like she understood confidently. Lilly always had a way with reading people. It worked all day for her. But by nightfall, her luck would have run out with this method, but her daylight adventures went without a hitch.

On her way back to the Inn for the evening, Lilly stopped by a small brook that was covered with a small bridge. She slipped off her shoes and let her feet dangle in the current. Instantly, it hit her. That sound. It was the water harp strumming ever so distantly in her ears. The babbling of the brook enhanced the sound to the point of almost being music. And there again, it was that other sound. It was almost a voice, distant and beautiful.

Splash!

A small child had tossed a stone into the brook, shattering Lilly's daydream. She smiled at the young boy as he grinned and dashed away in a run.

The sun was creeping toward the horizon. Lilly slipped her shoes back on and made her way back to the Wayfarer. She skipped along as her shoes clippity-clopped on the cobblestones. She wished she hadn't promised her parents she'd return so quickly. She had no idea what her travels would be like, and so far, these were all beyond her imagination. But tonight, yes tonight, she would learn to wash dishes and mop, whatever those might be. She had decided that even if it was hard work, it would be new work, and more importantly, new lessons in life.

She thought about how nice the bed would feel again tonight. She pictured herself spending a little more time on the rooftop stargazing, eyeing her special star named Kato.

Unfortunately, Kato was turning color.

15

The architecture of Stone Castle was far more impressive than met the eye. Long before a stone was laid, many secret passages and special rooms were planned. Certain windows and doors were placed directionally to the sun and moon phases. Still other passageways seemed forever locked unless the proper combination was known prior to the attempt to open. Years of planning and craftsmanship went into the building of this grand building.

The Hall of Enlightenment was one such room. It was a long and narrow, nearly vacant room. Elaborate murals were painstakingly painted throughout the room, including a giant mural of God upon the ceiling with his strong arm and hand extending out across the ceiling and partially down the left-hand wall.

The right side of the room was lit by ten round-topped windows with glass panes. As light entered these panes, it illuminated the opposite wall with ten sun-lit patterns the same shape as the window from which it came. These sunlight patterns landed upon ten beautifully stenciled and painted crests, each containing different subjects within.

Some crests had books, others had plants and flowers. Some donned moons and stars. To the untrained eye, these ornate and colorful crests seemed to be mere homages to the Literati group, but these were no mere homages. During the castle's building, ten enormously heavy stone doors were perfectly placed and hinged so that the touch of a finger could swing them open. On the outside of each door, there was a large metal cross that operated its mechanisms like a doorknob.

Behind each door was a steep stone staircase leading down to a lower room far beneath the castle's main floors. In each room was a raised stone pedestal with a large rock sarcophagus atop. Alongside this pedestal were other rock tables designed to hold candelabras and manuscripts. These stone rooms were to be the tombs of each Literati elder of the time.

The doors to these rooms had never been locked. Access was allowed for cleaning purposes by the younger students of the time. But once it was time for the sealing each tomb, the throwing of one lever from within would set in motion numerous gears and latches that could not be unlocked with only one exception.

On two consecutive days a year, the sun was positioned precisely in the sky to shed light directly upon a small hole in the door within the paintings of the crest. On those two days alone, the sunlight piercing this solar keyhole released the inner mechanisms and the large exterior cross could be turned, thusly allowing the door to once again be opened.

Today would be the first time in history that the latches would be tested for their original purpose.

Two lines of solemn Literati students and clergy made a path into the Hall of Enlightenment. Eight of the remaining Literati elders carried the body of Tolk onward to his prepared resting place. Ahead of the casket was Elias, now elder of his order.

Above of the crest of Tolk, his name had been painted, and the doorknob cross had his name etched into its surface. The casket temporarily came to rest at the head of the stone staircase. All bowed, and Elias began the ceremony.

Per Tolk's request, a collection of scriptures was to be read. Some were philosophical quotes, and others were of a more spiritual nature. Some scriptures were read from scrolls of ancient manuscripts on Christianity. The final words of scripture read were actually lyrics of a poem Tolk had written for this very occasion. His eloquent words were recited.

Like the lovely flowers laid, how soon the
precious petals fade.

And called hence from Earthly gloom, now these
buds can fully bloom.

When the ceremony was complete, Tolk's body was carried down the steep steps and placed into its sarcophagus and sealed shut. Large stacks of Tolk's original manuscripts were placed alongside, each having been copied and placed in the vast library of the castle. One by one, young and old of this elite group were granted one trip into the room to pay their final respects. Elias was the last to leave. He threw the large lever of the door lock, triggering its internal gears into action. With a final bow of his head and a tender prayer, Elias pulled the door closed. Ratcheting and clanking noises could be heard within. The last thump of the lock hit home. Its sound echoed through the Hall of Enlightenment with an eerie finality. The ceremony was complete. Per tradition, all recited in unison.

"Lay down thy burdens, great elder! Long live Literati!"

16

The same sun had long-since set in Cobblestone as it had miles away at Stone Castle. Lilly had learned how to clean and mop quite well with Margarite's instruction. Margarite realized that her first assessments of this young girl were well off-target. In two short days, she had grown fond of Lilly and liked having her around. She'd asked Lilly to share some stories from home. Margarite had never traveled north farther than the outskirts of town, and Lilly's stories intrigued her.

"Ever thought 'bout stayin', Lassy? 'Tis a nice town, Cobblestone. Reckon I like yer work ethic, see? Could use a hand 'round this place, ya know?"

"I'm flattered, Margarite. Really, I am. You've been so very nice to me and helped me so. I cannot stay, but I will most definitely return one day, hopefully with my family. They shouldn't live the rest of their lives without tasting your bread! My, it's so wonderful!"

"Ya don't have ta keep kissin' me rear 'bout me bread rolls. I'll be sendin' some home with ya!"

Lilly chuckled. "May I go to my room now. I want to reflect on my day and look at the stars a while."

Margarite agreed to her request and gave her a bowl of water for bathing. She also handed her a leftover biscuit from her midday crowd. "You'll be a wantin' this after yer star gazin' on the rooftop."

Lilly smiled even wider as she spun to leave. Over her shoulder she chirped, "I'll never be able to repay you, Marge."

Margarite smiled inwardly. She whispered quietly to herself. "You already have, little lady. If ya don't eat me into the poorhouse."

* * *

Lilly cleaned up and put on her robe. It felt soft against her skin as she gazed out the window into the sky. She hoisted herself out onto the rooftop and sat down. Again, the sky was as full as Lilly's head and heart. She was alarmed to see that her star was much too evident in the sky. It was larger and now it had turned nearly red.

"Whatever could be changing my star?" she whispered.

It was a strange sight, seeing a star change color … and getting bigger to boot! She was a bit unsettled by the star's new looks, but let it go, blaming the city lanterns for its changes.

She'd spent nearly an hour reliving her day in town, going over it all again and again. Her eyes were starting to droop as she shuffled back through the window's opening. Before hopping into bed, she took one last glance into the sky. She shook her head.

"I must be sleepy. I swear that star keeps getting bigger."

Lilly *was* sleepy, and that star was surely getting bigger.

* * *

Meanwhile, many other eyes were glued to the sky and that same star. The Literati had sent the signal to Cobblestone Castle that the time was near, assuming that the king had sent word through the city for all to prepare.

He had not. He had taken Tolk's last words quite literally.

The King's men were poised and ready for what may come … with a small band of sentinels ready to mount their steeds to gather word on wherever and however the meteor would land.

The Literati were nervously staring at the night sky, NOT taking Tolk's last words about the meteor lightly. Worry plagued them all.

Those near the Iceland Pool were also looking up, pondering what was happening with Lilly's star. Why so large and red?

Some of Cobblestone's townspeople were stargazing, too. Many of those staring elected to stay awake a little longer just to see what was going on in the sky.

Animals in barn stalls across the city were unsettled. The light rain and pale clouds did little to comfort them.

Lilly was nearly asleep when the first sprinkles of rain began to fall outside her window. Ah, there it was again … the water harp. Trickling tunes. It was that quiet, distant, watery voice so soft and lovely. The light drips of rain sent her into a deep sleep.

It was the calm before the storm—a storm like nothing any had ever seen before.

17

Most meteors burn up as they enter the Earth's atmosphere. The immense heat disintegrates the foreign rock before it has a chance to make impact. Particles sometimes fall to Earth without notice. Dust balls and smoke dissipate unseen.

Not this meteor. The giant ball of burning mass was enormous. As it raced through space, bits of fiery lava were spat into the emptiness. Still, it flew onward with a nearly endless amount of fuel for its fire. It was a ball of hell fire on a mission.

Well past midnight, the weary eyes that had prayed against hope that the meteor would disperse were now assured of its destiny. Larger and larger it grew in the sky, and its intensity only glowed brighter. Even with the now-forming clouds of light rain, it's color could easily be seen through it all. Distant thunder could be barely heard rolling far away.

Three hours before sunrise, the noise began. It was an endless far-away roar that echoed along with the storm cloud thunder creeping closer. As the roar came nearer, other sounds of explosions and crackles could be discerned. It all was thunderously loud, and vibrations could be felt in the earth. The surface of the Iceland Pool vibrated into waves. The foundations of Cobblestone Castle began to vibrate with the loud rumble. New slate shingles from the rooftop of Stone Castle cracked and slid to the ground.

By now, every living creature knew that something was dreadfully wrong.

As the meteor raced through the Earth's atmosphere, large chunks of burning rock jettisoned from its outer crust. Nearly a third of the meteor broke away and flew deep into the northern Dark Lands to places still unfound, setting fire to large deadwood forests. Another large splinter of rock shards broke away and exploded over Troll Country setting ablaze most of its entirety.

Many more pieces continued to break away from the burning mass, decreasing its size, but none of its ferocity and speed. Hundreds of burning shards of comet scattered through both the Deep Forest and the City of Cobblestone. The forest burned red and homes and buildings in the city had caught fire. Everywhere there was fire and smoke.

Still, the meteor raged on. Even with the loss of its outer shell, the meteor was at least fifty yards wide and immeasurably potent.

People of the village near the Iceland Pool were huddled together bracing for the worst. It seemed as if the meteor would crash right through their home. Fear and shock shook them all, and they knew full well that their scant shelter of trees was no match for the fiery sun that was being cast toward them.

Widespread panic had engulfed Cobblestone. Some frantically tried to put out fires, choking on the black smoke that filled the air. Some houses were beginning to fall, enraged in fire. Screams and cries for help pierced the air.

Lilly woke in shock to the horror outside her window. As far as she could see, there were homes ablaze and smoke choked the city. She quickly grabbed her cloak from off the rooftop and scooped up her belongings. She raced downstairs to find Margarite steering everyone outdoors in case the fire should reach the inn. She ran outside and down the steps not knowing where to go or what to do. Overhead in the sky was the most frightening thing she'd ever seen. Her very own star was now a giant glowing bomb about to hit nearby. Through the smoke she could see the orange outline of the Iceland Peak reflecting the plummeting meteor behind it. She shrieked as a wave of worry flashed through her head and heart. Her family! Before she could muster another thought, the next occurrence chilled her to the bone.

The meteor had made first impact.

18

The eyes of many from Stone Castle to Cobblestone stared in shock, just seconds before first impact.

Like a bullet from Hell, the meteor careened toward the peak of Iceland. An enormous explosion shook the earth as the meteor crashed THROUGH the peak. Rocks, ice, earth and fire ejected from the mountain top, flying miles from what was once the peak, removing the entire top of the snowy crest.

But the meteor wasn't finished yet.

As debris flew through the air, the meteor still plummeted downward, sliding down the steep slope, carving a channel through the forest highlands. Fires erupted from what was left of the carnage behind the meteor, still glowing as it tore away the Earth's surface.

Down, down it slid, burning, biting, killing everything in its path, still showing no signs of slowing down or burning out. Through the smoke and chaos it slid until there was no place to go but straight into the soil in the bottom of the valley.

As it pierced the Earth's surface, another shockwave blast shook the forest and city. Onward it pressed down into the bedrock, burning the stone with both heat and pressure as it delved. Crystalized remains of rock and soil smoldered and burned inside the tunnel bored by the meteor. With a loud screech of rock on rock, the meteor slowed its pace and came to a stop, still sizzling and crackling in its deep hole.

It was then that another shocking event took place.

An immeasurably bright light flashed above in the night sky, and with it came a clap of thunder as loud as the meteor crash itself, shaking the ground.

And then the rain…

The sky dumped water so hard that it hit the ground with a splash like a tidal wave. More rain fell and fell and still fell.

Many forest fires were extinguished in seconds. Houses in Cobblestone began to smolder and steam. The mote around Cobblestone Castle began to overflow its banks, creeping into the lower stores of the castle, flooding the carefully prepared goods the king had ordered to be stored there.

Across the forest, the floors of Stone Castle sloshed with water running through the huge building.

Everywhere—water, steam, and a few fires still burning through it all.

Amid the chaos stood Lilly outside the inn, too scared to move. The shock of it all had chills locking her spine. People ran past her in a panic. Many others were climbing the steps of the inn to escape the rising water. Lilly stepped backward into them and up onto the first step, still shaking and now crying. All of her earthly possessions were beneath her arms, soaking wet.

Somehow, through the raging mess before her, a sound was heard by her and her alone. It was that same sound that comforted her throughout her entire life. In the middle of this horrendous storm, she still heard the water. She still felt the water. That distant water harp tone was seeping into her ears. And finally, that familiar, quiet, dripping voice came to her. She could make out no words, but it was there—somehow soothing her heart despite the horrible predicament encircling her.

As she listened, oblivious to her surroundings, she took notice of the ground. Yes, the water was moving past quickly, but that was not what caught her eye. The water was moving in a different direction than downhill! Some streams were moving sideways, some uphill, and other pools were simply rising. As each pool reached the crest of its edges, the overflow would flow away all in the same general direction as the rest of the flood. All of the water—after overflowing—was traveling north.

Water was flowing to the heart of the Deep Forest. Most definitely, it was rolling toward the initial blast from only minutes ago.

It was flowing to the meteor.

19

The waters of the Iceland Pool were rising fast. The people of Lilly's village were grabbing belongings—and each other—and climbing the hillside as fast as possible. Some had been burned from the raging fires along the hillside, but they pressed on with as much fortitude as they could muster. Shouts and cries added to the panic. Darkness engulfed them all as they tried to maneuver the treacherous hillside.

Lilly's parents found each other in the darkness only to realize their worst fear.

"Where's Kato?"

They were in no place to search for anything or anyone in this total darkness, but the sun would soon be rising. They continued to call, but the entanglement of countless other voices made it impossible to hear any response.

The wait until daybreak was heartbreaking. Kato's parents could only hold one another crying. Words of comfort were of no use. Time stood still.

Wet, cold, scared, and depressed, the village waited in the dark, fearful of what the light might bring.

* * *

Daylight on the steep hillside showed an unrecognizable Iceland Pool. Its banks were never larger. Its waters never so deep. It was determined that the water table was slowly receding, but it was of little comfort to those who were frantically searching for loved ones.

Two hours after daylight, Kato was still nowhere to be found. So far, it appeared that all others were accounted for except for him. Another child about his age had been found but was across the large cove over a hundred yards away. The child was unhurt, but it was now a waiting game for him as well. He would have to remain where he was until the currents slowed enough to swim.

Kato's father began a more extensive search. The hillside where they were curved away behind them into a long cove stretching southward. The hillside was slow-going. Briars and rocks made travel difficult, but he continued his search with fortitude, calling out Kato's name often.

Kato's father was at wit's end. He was just about to fall to his knees and wale in sorrow when he called aloud another time. This time, to his utter joy, he heard a reply.

A hundred yards offshore was a floating tree trunk swirling in the slight current. Sitting comfortably on top was Kato, his hand waving at his father.

"I'm okay, Poppa," he called. "The water saved me."

"Hold on tight, Kato," he shouted. "I'll find something that floats and come get you!"

"No need, Poppa," Kato yelled again. "The water will bring me to you. It'll bring me home on this log."

"We can't be sure, Kato! I'll come get you!"

"I told you, Poppa. The water saved me. The water will bring me home on this log."

"Kato, what are you talking about?" he shouted.

"It's the water, Poppa."

"It told me so."

20

Two hours after the initial dumping of rain, the storm passed as quickly as it came, but not before wreaking havoc far and wide.

Waters were still high and rushing as daylight arrived. Light of day only showed more carnage. Some houses were gone, and other buildings had people on the roofs calling for help—the rest of the house flooded beneath them.

The extra stores of food at Cobblestone Castle were mostly ruined. Fruit and vegetables were salvaged, but much of what the king had stored was ruined. He had grossly misjudged the impact of the meteor. In his haste to search the impact sight, his greed to find treasure had cost him a far greater price. His city was in shambles. People had died. There was little food left for those who had survived. His handling of the whole ordeal was a complete and utter failure, and he knew it deep inside. There was no time for treasure hunting now. His city needed everything he could give them, and then some. His treasure hunting squad was now a search party for the dead and wounded. Water was still flooded across the city. Nothing was passable.

The king's men began salvaging what they could from the stores, and the king sent Lock with a message for Stone Castle. "Our city is destroyed".

* * *

Water levels were subsiding in Stone Castle. No one was injured, and most of their wares and stores were safe. Elias addressed his fellow Literati.

"Cleaning is now paramount, men, for soon we shall prepare to barricade the doors in case of intrusion. Be watchful for both those in need and for dangerous people. We must be ready instantly if something should occur. Shark, Daniel, prepare your weaponry for use. Let us pray we will not need to use it."

All did as they were told, and all worried about the wellbeing of others and of how they had survived the night. The unknowing was rattling their minds, and most prayed as they worked with many unknowns clouding their thoughts.

How widespread could this catastrophe have reached?

21

In the two hours before daylight, the civilians of Cobblestone were still in a panic trying to assess damages in the darkness and steamy fog shrouding the city.

Margarite's workers had scoured the Inn for fire and water damage. The Inn and several of the nearby buildings had been spared of serious repercussions from the storm and meteor fires. Damages were slight to the structures, but the townsfolk and walking wounded were filing into any building to find dry shelter. The Inn quickly transformed into a storm shelter, it's dining hall now covered with blankets and countless people nursing one another in the aftermath.

Lilly had been helping direct people up the steps and trying to find a location for them all. It was organized chaos at best, but there was comfort for many as they settled into the Inn and waited for the rising sun to show the carnage of the city.

As the sun was just beginning to show light upon Cobblestone, Lilly stood on the front steps of the Inn, her belongings at her feet. Tears were still flowing from her eyes as she looked toward the sunrise. Soon,

Margarite stepped out of the front doors and looked to her new friend with a knowing glance of respect.

"Lassy," she stated. "You don't have to say it. I know you'll be taking leave. I understand."

Lilly's teary eyes looked back at Margarite. "I have to go. My family … I … I have to check on them. My God, it could be bad. I … I have to go."

"Do what you gotta do, Lassy."

"Margarite," Lilly whimpered. "I can never repay you for all you've done for me."

Margarite nodded in agreement, trying to push a smile past her own tears. She knew full well that this young lady's heart was breaking. Her own was breaking as well. She'd grown very fond of Lilly in the past few days. It was an uncommon friendship that grew quickly out of trust and compassion. Margarite spoke up again.

"You go on, girly, but you better be comin' back to see me. You still owe me a few floor scrubbin's."

Lilly raced to Margarite, embracing her into a deep hug as she cried. "I'm coming back … I'm coming back. I don't know when, but I'm coming back. I gotta go …"

She pulled away from Margarite and tucked her belongings under her arms. She mustered one last smile and stepped off the steps of the Inn. In seconds, she was in a dead run, splashing water as she ran. The Old Road was a long and twisted path before her. Over a hundred miles lie between her and the banks of the Iceland Pool … and her family.

"Dear Lord," she whimpered. "Let them be safe!"

22

By early morning, King Marcus had surmised that he'd misjudged Tolk's last words. His city was a mess. This meteor had done its share of damage. Despite the harm done to many buildings, there were fewer deaths than the carnage would show. There were many townspeople injured with burns and abrasions, but those were being treated in a makeshift hospital in the center of town.

The water had receded as quickly as it came. The widespread damage it had caused still left mud and residue as far as the eye could see. The stench of smoldering ash and steam plagued the air. This ugly scene would take weeks or even months resurrect. The water had done as much damage as the fires, but it seemed that the rains were a blessing … being a means to an end to the fires. But still, the muddy remains of such a storm caused its share of wrath as well. Where there wasn't ash, there was mud.

No one seemed to notice where the waters were flowing. Perhaps only Lilly noticed the direction of their travels. At this point, the fact that the water was going away was enough to please them. In a less disastrous time, maybe it would have been noticed that the water was flowing north toward the meteor site. It might have been noted that something truly special was happening. But, that was not the case. Too many other distractions clouded the surroundings of Cobblestone. The direction of water travel was the least of their worries.

King Marcus had abandoned his treasure hunt for jewels for the time being. The thought still teased his mind, and he still kept that secret to himself, knowing that eventually the time would come for him to make that journey and investigate where that fiery meteor came to land. Those were thoughts for another day. Now, his city and his people needed all of his efforts. He would rethink his pursuits in a few weeks when some semblance of normalcy returned.

King Marcus, by most measurable means, was a fair and just king. Despite his love of jewels and power, he still cared very much for his realm of Greenwale. He kept communications open via his Tower Ravens between Stone Castle, Blue Haven, and the Bay of Greenwale. He considered his farthings a Utopia of sorts. He and his queen would often take leisurely walks throughout the city, taking time to visit with the townsfolk and partaking in the wondrous foods served up in the city's various establishments. The Wayfarer Inn was a common stop for them, enjoying Margarite's wondrous breads and special meats. The king and queen took time in their city, and it made a difference. Cobblestone thrived because of them.

So, the king's thoughts were rightfully focused on the wellbeing of his realm. Rebuilding was paramount. Greenwale must be restored. That was his foremost thought.

But jewels still stirred in his mind …

23

Mid-morning after the meteor crash, the halls of Stone Castle were drying. They, too, had the aftermath of mud and water damage within the building. But, by and large, the Literati had faired the storm well. Their early planning and precautions had served them well.

The team of three members was anxious to start their trek to see the meteor crash site, but the elders had properly instructed them to postpone that venture until it was proven that the castle was safe from intrusion. Also, it was unknown if any travelers in need might also happen along needing assistance. Collectively, they elected to let the mud settle, at least for a few days.

After all, day one of this meteor's crash was more than enough to behold.

* * *

The first day after the meteor crash proved uneventful with cleaning being the first priority. The water system flowing through the castle had overflowed its bounds but did not cause more damage other than mud residue. It was now a waiting game to see how the rest of the nearby world survived.

It didn't take long for some of the aftermath to show itself. The fears of troll encounters would be realized sooner than the Literati expected. Although the Literati were unaware, the flaming portions of the meteor that scattered into troll country had set ablaze virtually all of its countryside. The rains had not fallen there as heavily as it had in Cobblestone and nearby communities. Troll country was scorched along with its residents. Little remained of that already crude and rough civilization. Trolls were on the move, searching for food and shelter in any way they could muster. And when trolls muster … nothing good happens.

24

Lilly was on a dead run as she splashed through puddles and streams flowing over the Old Road. She had paused to catch her breath several times, but she raced forward with all the fortitude she could manage. She desperately wanted to put as many miles beneath her as possible. She'd passed the water spring that had saved her only days before, still pressing forward.

She had pulled out her father's map and could tell by the graphics that she would be finding Stone Castle in the early morning. She had no idea what that would entail, but it was a mark on her map that took her closer to home. Somewhere beyond that castle was a trail marked that led toward her home … northward near the Iceland Pool. By now, she had evaluated the lay of the land and had a certain sense of her proximity. The sun passing overhead had given her a clue directionally.

But her pressing problem now was hunger. She hadn't eaten since the day before, and her stomach was aching with the lack of food. Darkness was falling, and there was no food to be eaten.

She still pressed onward in the near darkness knowing that she would have to bed down and rest soon. Hunger would have to wait until some semblance of daylight could help her find mushrooms or snails to fill the void.

Two hours after nightfall, Lilly stopped her pace. She nestled into a small thicket of trees. She pulled her woven cloak around her and hid amongst the saplings. Her mind still wanted to run, but her body had given out. Her muscles ached from the run, and her stomach still wanted food badly. The means came to an end, and she gave up. Her body settled into rest, and her mind gave way to sleep. Tomorrow would be another day. Sleep needed to happen. Maybe there would be food found tomorrow.

As sleep pulled her under, her mind still raced with worry about her family. Did the meteor destroy her village? Did her family live? Was there any semblance of her community still left after such a disaster?

Many questions still loomed in her mind, but sleep finally overtook her. A much-needed rest consumed her, and for the moment, she was content.

The road to home was long, indeed.

25

Lilly woke with a start along the Old Road. Her body was quite sore from her hard run the day before. The Old Road was quiet this morning, but it did not help Lilly's sense of impending rush. She must hurry on her way.

Waking and stretching, Lilly was quickly reminded of her hunger from the night before. Starvation alone was worrisome enough for her, and her lack of knowledge of the roads and trails ahead only added to the fear she held in her heart. Perhaps there would be mushrooms along the road at some point.

Bracing herself for her journey, she leapt into a jog, forcing her sore muscles to cooperate. Unbeknownst to her, Stone Castle wasn't far from her resting place the night before. An hour into her run, the slate rooftop of Stone Castle came into view. She wasn't sure if she should creep by in her cloak or take a chance stopping at the place that she had feared growing up, eerie tales from her youth coming forward in her mind. The Literati were scary figments in her memory, and she wasn't sure how to handle her current predicament. She was basically lost and desperately hungry for food of some sort. Her hunger outweighed her fears as she slowed her pace and came to a stop in front of the great stone building before her. It was remarkably pretty, even in the wet conditions that muddied everything. The slate shingles, the gloriously-colored curtains dangling in the breeze; the grandeur of this special building captivated her.

Alone she stood in her woven cloak, taking in all the sights and sounds.

"Who might you be?" asked a bold voice of a young man standing just outside the castle. "You look out of sorts."

Lilly was startled by his comments and stared dumbfounded at the lad before her, being overly cautious. She dared not speak, sizing up this young man before her. He was a striking lad with a demeanor that seemed pleasant, but Lilly was still not comfortable with his address. The fellow's smile was comforting, and it eased Lilly's concern. She walked closer, still not speaking or acknowledging his address.

The lad spoke up again.

"You CAN speak, can you not?"

Lilly's anger arose. She finally uttered a growl, "Yes, I can speak."

"Well, that helps matters," he exclaimed. "Wait, you are one of those Wild Folk, aren't you?"

Lilly's blood boiled. "WE ARE NOT WILD! What is it with you city folk? We dress differently, and you consider us WILD. Ugh, the nerve!"

The young man chuckled to himself. "You're feisty, I'll give you that."

"I hear that a lot," she frowned.

Lilly could not help being somewhat soothed by the lad's demeanor. He was confident and calm, even professional in his nature. His dark hair and deep brown eyes were quite captivating, even in this strange encounter. His smile stirred her within, and she was not quite sure how to respond. She calmed herself and spoke again.

"I … umm …" she stammered. "I need assistance. I'm lost and I'm starving." She stared at the ground, not making eye contact. She pondered her next sentence.

"Is there anyway you could help? I … I need to get back to my family. I'm dreadfully worried about them. They are of the Iceland Pool. I don't know the way."

The lad seemed satisfied with her response. His smile still beamed, and Lilly felt awkward in his presence. Something about his smile reached deep inside her. The shaky ground between them settled, and he offered his hand to her.

Lilly extended her hand to his. It was a practice she'd noticed in Cobblestone. People would grab hands as an address or perhaps a term of affection. It was commonplace with the city folk to greet one another in this fashion, so she did her best to oblige.

When he took her hand, she felt a wash of emotions she'd never felt before. His hand was warm and firm. Her small palm melted into his, as he gently squeezed firm. It somehow felt like a hug from family, only far more intense in this moment. Time stopped for only a few seconds during that handshake, but it made a huge impression on her. She'd never felt a connection like that before. It was a foreign, but special feeling. There was a tug-of-war between her heart and mind, and it touched her within. Concentration was difficult for that few seconds, but she pulled it back together and continued her response.

"Are you … you … one of the Literati?" she asked.

"Oh no," he responded. "I have not yet attained that status. I'm here to learn. Perhaps one day I will be held in such high regard. I am Squire Daniel … at your service!"

Lilly blushed with his statement. People of her village were kind to one another, but this man's cordial presence had her thoughts pulled somewhere between flattery and respect.

Maybe Cobblers aren't so bad.

"I really need to find my way back to my village. I'm so very hungry. I only have a few coins to offer for food. Its not much, but I'm so very hungry."

Daniel's smile beamed. "You'll have to meet the elders first, but I'm sure they will find some bread and cheese to fill you up."

"Oh, my! You have bread! I could eat the cow it's made from!"

Daniel only chuckled at her response. "I'm pretty sure bread is not made from cows, but we have some left over from breakfast. And these elder Literati aren't as hard-nosed as their reputation eludes. I think you'll find them welcoming."

Lilly was indeed welcomed by the elders of the Literati. Her recount of the happenings of Cobblestone during the meteor crash held them mesmerized. They had not yet heard word from Cobblestone, even by raven, so her words were precious to them. She told of the fiery blazes from the sky and even remarked of the strange movements of the waters from the rainfall. The fires made sense to them, but the water movement seemed to fall on deaf ears. That watery figment of her imagination was of little account to them. Water doesn't run uphill, so that part of her story was discounted.

Lilly had filled her stomach and her pouches with an abundance of food. She had quizzed them all over the best passage back to her village, gleaning descriptions of the Old Road and the paths that led away from it toward her home. She felt rushed to be on her way but found a fondness toward the Literati Elders and their all-knowing mannerisms about everything she could ask. Her brief stay left her with a strong feeling of compassion and wisdom toward them. She'd thanked them many times over and vowed to visit again someday during better times. She was just gathering her things to leave when something outside drew everyone's attention.

It was Shark racing in through the front doors.

"We have a problem!"

Outside on The Old Road, two travelers stomped forward to the castle front doors. The watchers that would have been on guard had been preoccupied with Lilly's visit. Somehow, these two visitors had nearly walked right up to the doors without an address.

These were no mere passersby. These were two trolls that had made their way south after the meteor fires had ravaged the lands north of Stone Castle. Their clothing was darkened with soot, and their moods were equally ugly to their appearance. These two were not here to ask for help. They were here to take all they could by force.

Part of troll nature is their frightening demeanor. A common misconception is that they are big oafs with little intelligence. That is not the case. Part of the fear they instill is their intelligent speech. If their size was not enough to shake a soul, their eloquent verbiage could make one feel outsmarted even before their immensity loomed above. Fear was always their strong suit, and they wore it well ... *and* ... reasoning was out-the-window before speech ever began.

Their fists pounded on the wooden doors.

Boom, boom!

"Open up, ye brilliant fellows! We know you saw this disaster coming. You have a store of food pilfered away. We are here to partake!"

Within seconds, two large beams were pressed against the front doors. Several Literati scattered to predetermined locations and took up arms for protection.

Elias, now elder of the group, spoke up.

"We will give you food to survive. We will not bow down to your intrusion."

"Intrusion?" shouted one of the trolls. "You should welcome us! The alternative could get ugly."

Silence ensued for only a moment. The trolls took no time for bantering wits. Their aim was to break down the door and take what they wished, bashing anyone in their way.

Lilly stood paralyzed along the wall. This certainly was not in her travel plans of racing home. Daniel stood by her side, pulling her close. He gave knowing glances to others nearby, cuing them to take position for battle. The Literati had taken precautions with calculated precision. This situation was not going to end well.

Boom, boom! The sound rattled Lilly to the core.

The walls rumbled with the pounds of the troll's shoulders.

Boom, boom!

The walls shook. The beams against the doors rattled, still holding their position.

Just as both trolls prepared to slam against the doors another time, something above them had eluded them.

It was Shark. He held a very heavy rock in his hands and thrust it downward, centering one of the troll's heads, breaking his neck in a split second. The body of the troll collapsed into a pile, quivering and shaking violently.

The remaining troll turned his attention upward, expecting another stone to fall. To his dismay, another stone was not his worry. The contents of a large tub of oil emptied above him, dousing his entire body and the ground around him. As the troll tried to gain his senses, shaking oil from his skin, a lone arrow released from up above. It's flaming tip hitting hard, but did more damage with its flame.

Instantly the troll was set ablaze. He scrambled to put out the fire, but it was too late. His body sizzled and scorched alongside his counterpart lying dead beside him. It all happened so fast. From forceful mayhem to scorching death … all in a matter of seconds.

The Literati had protected themselves well, but it was an ugly and sad ending. Two trolls lie dead and burning on their front doorstep. In a place of schooling, an education was displayed that no one present would forget. Outside this castle of highest learning, the lowest of deaths prevailed. Justified murder is still a wretched thing to behold.

* * *

Lilly still stood shaking against the wall, appalled by what she'd never experienced before … raw death of a living being right before her eyes.

All of the vague things her parents had told her about the perils of the outside world seemed to be playing out before her eyes. She had witnessed such wondrous things. She'd been a part of a lifestyle that was so new and exciting. Life was exploding around her. Only now, the rawness of the world was hitting home. Death. Burning. Floods. Chaos. Fear.

Perhaps Mother was right. The great side was more than great. The bad side was more than bad. She realized that she had thrown herself into the big mix, and it was more than she'd bargained for. Big life was really, really big.

The stench of the burning aftermath with the trolls seeped through the halls of stone castle. The remaining flames were extinguished with douses of flour. Several of the Literati began the clean-up outside, fabricating large stretchers to drag the trolls. The men did not have to drag them far. As usual, the Literati had thought of everything. In the distance stood a pile of wooden rubble just outside the courtyard. The trolls were rolled on top and jostled into place.

There would be yet another fire today. The incineration of the trolls was more than necessary. It would accomplish several things.

For one, trolls were known for carrying disease. Most were not something that would harm humans, but it was still necessary to rid the forest of as much as possible. The fire would also keep the stench of rotting flesh from filling the air in all directions. Also, it was hoped among the Literati that such a display would serve as an omen to future unwanted guests. Even as rotten as trolls could be, this highly recognizable display would be understood at first glance. It certainly would not scare them away, but it might deter a wiser troll from meeting a similar demise. But mostly, the Literati knew that it was the only honorable thing to do in such a sad predicament. Honor seemed a far cry from what these two trolls deserved, but it was what made the Literati worthy of taking up such actions against an aggressor. It was the right means to a wrong end.

As things began to settle at the castle, Lilly came to the realization that this road to home could be far more dangerous than she had anticipated. *What if there were more trolls? Even if I hid, they'd smell me! How will I get home?*

The Literati were thinking the same.

Elais' voice could be heard. "Shark, Daniel. A word, please."

Daniel released his embrace and followed Elias. Shark, too, followed. Lilly wasn't sure she wanted Daniel to leave her side. His embrace had been her only comfort during the troll attack. Plus, something inside her felt safe near him. She found herself wanting to be near him more. She shook the thought from her head. *How ridiculous. Wake up, Lilly. He's just another special person on this twisted journey I've chosen.*

Soon, Shark and Daniel returned from their meeting with Elias. As both men walked past Lilly toward their back chambers, Daniel spoke to her.

"Wait here. I'll be back in a moment."

Lilly was perplexed. Half of her was impatient to leave, and the other half was petrified of what might happen if she did. She began to pace nervously as she waited, mulling over the consequences of each choice. She knew that the only thing certain was that one of those two things had to happen, and it needed to happen fast. Nightfall was only a couple of hours away, and she had hoped to be much closer to home by now, wherever that was.

Just as Lilly was about to call for an Elder, Shark and Daniel emerged from the hall, each carrying a shoulder satchel and an empty pouch. Daniel gave her a quick glance.

"We need some provisions. Be right back."

Lilly wasn't sure what that meant. Again she found herself waiting for something and had no idea what it was. She was again growing impatient when the two stepped back into the room. They both stood before her with determined expressions on their faces.

Shark spoke first. "Ma'am, Elias informed me to tell you what little we know about the Iceland Pool. He has sent the Tower Ravens to fly over for a visual. The waters are receding considerably. The meteor missed the south shores."

Lilly gave a gasp or relief. "That's where my family is!"

"I know," spoke Shark again. "Although the Ravens speak only a few words of English, Elias has grown to know much of their language. Although the Wild … uh … your folk are difficult to decern from the air, there is at least some human life along those shores."

"Oh …" Lilly's voice trailed off, and her eyes swelled with tears. "Thank you for letting me know. I've been so worried."

"We know that as well, Miss Riverpool. We also know that the road before you could be perilous, and you are not familiar with the paths."

She peered up at the two men before her. "I'm scared."

The two men glanced at one another and smiled.

Each spoke their names aloud, then they both bowed and in unison spoke again.

"At your service!"

26

Some fifty miles northeast of Stone Castle, the waters of the Iceland Pool were trying desperately to recede. Many landslides of mud had slid from its shores and into the murky depths of this giant lake of dismay. This reservoir's only outlet was the raging North Fork River, rushing its way eastward toward The Green Sea, far north of the Bay of Greenwale.

The banks of the North Fork River were being pounded with near tidal wave flows. This sometimes-placid river had seen more water in two days than it had in three months prior. Huge boulders had been ripped from its banks as trees and other huge debris crashed and tore its way downstream. What few trees that had survived the initial blasts now resembled eerie skeletons forlornly peering down at the carnage below—their limbs crammed full of still more debris high above the current water levels where the water had crested the day before. The carcasses of dead animals were jammed into these limbs as if the trees had taken mercy upon them and scooped them up in pity. Although parts of Greenwale were emerging from this disaster, the North Fork River was still enduring the blunt of everything that upstream had washed away. It was if the battle was over, but the fighting still continued. For over a hundred miles of this river's travels, only death and destruction followed.

Far upstream to the east of the Iceland Pool, The East Fork River was flushing what remained of Troll Country. Stench and mire abounded there. An ugliness unfitting of the forest existed in this rough country some fifty miles across. Most of this land lied in the northeastern portions of Greenwale and were the usual confines of the troll community. They preferred it far away from most of mankind and kept their filth and dismay located there. The greenery of the forest tolerated troll-kind well, but the animal creatures steered far away, knowing that only death awaited them there. The trolls were formidable hunters, and what few living creatures that still resided there were quite crafty to the nature of the trolls, being ever watchful of their movements. Most of these other living creatures were equally nasty to the trolls.

Trolls of this era were still somewhat abundant. In the decades that followed, the trolls slowly declined to extinction. It was a perplexing dilemma these detestable creatures succumbed to. Their extinction was inevitable, and even the trolls saw it coming with little they could do to turn the tables. The issue they faced was at the forefront of their every day. Extinction comes from the lack of perpetuation. That was their fate. They were strong enough to endure almost any climate or situational conflict. They were healthy enough to sustain themselves for over a full lifetime of over one hundred years. Quite simply, they just could not sustainably reproduce.

Their reproduction cycle was not the issue. Many trolls were born into the world every season, usually in late springtime. Although they mated much like humans, a certain drive around springtime seemed to happen. Since the gestation period of troll-kind is about one year, each spring what scant few females left to give birth did just that.

That was the real problem. There were very few females. It's a social situation that could be studied by the greatest minds. The study of this one dilemma would fill volumes of literature. It was quite indicative of troll demeanor. Such bitterness and jealousy filled the hearts of every troll in the attempts to save their own kind. All males would strive to gain the hand of a female, but very few ever would. It was a ten-to-one ratio of males to females, so competition was fierce with a ninety percent chance of failure for most males. Ugly battles were fought over single females. Depression, anguish, and despair followed every battle and every broken heart. Anger and rage were the usual outcomes in life for any male to grow into and grow old in thereafter.

Then there was the female's side of the coin. She had an endless amount of suiters constantly hounding her for her hand. Even after taking her male, still other males would battle for her and her mating rights. This could appear to be beneficial, even pleasing for the female, but that was not the case. From the very month she was old enough to mate, she was not only expect to do so, but often forced. Even with suiters all around her begging for her love and bringing gifts of all sorts, she could never get a minute's peace in her long and pregnant life. As soon as her body healed from one baby, it was time to start again, hoping against hope for a baby girl and rarely achieving that goal—and even at that, it was a disheartening sight for a mother to watch her baby girl growing into womanhood, knowing full well the misery that awaited her.

Therein lies the fowl bitterness and hate that sours the troll soul. It was that never-ending plight of never getting what one wants. So, it was with this nature of being that the trolls took what they could from others whenever and wherever they could. That was usually by force accompanied with torture. If they could not have it, they wanted no one else to have it either.

It was an ugly system, but the system survived for as many generations as the trolls.

Some say mankind shares those traits.

Far north of the Iceland Pool were the formidable and eerie Dark Lands. Only rumors and folklore made up its history. Children's tales told of the sorcery of wizards and screeches of dragons lurking under the ominous dark clouds that loomed above its snowy peaks. Dark and dastardly things did live there, but no one ever dared to make the journey, or if they did, they never lived to return. It, too, was being flushed, melting nasty things from its ice and snow. Foul things. Its mud was black and smelled of death. Large portions of it silted into its waters and flowed downstream along the banks of what was known as No Man's Fork.

And it was aptly named.

* * *

Although the southern shores of the Iceland Pool had favored better than the rest, its inhabitants faced their share of woe, too. Lilly's village was mostly destroyed, but its civilians were able to begin picking up the pieces of their lives along the shore. As the water table dropped, other sections of their village would surface. Clean-up of that section would be a team effort, finding what they could of what once was. It was utterly sad, especially for one couple and their young son, Kato. Their family had survived the wreckage, but their hearts were still lost in worry about their precious daughter. All they could do is hope and pray that she, too, survived that horrid night. They plodded along, doing their best to help others dig through the rubble. As day's last light was falling on the second day after the disaster, the misery all around them could not match their worry inside.

Busy work is but a slight distraction for a broken heart.

27

Day two saw Cobblestone's civilians rallying together for one another. Families helped families clean up water damages and helped still others sift through the rubble of burned homes. Though very sad, the city overall had fared reasonably well considering what it had endured. The king's men had cleared most of the mud from the streets and resurfaced the dirt roads leading in and out of the city. The stores of food in the warehouses around town were opened to the public rationing its goods out to those in need. All totaled, nine people died and some thirty had injuries mostly consisting of burns.

Margarite had opened the Inn as a shelter for those who'd lost their homes. She also tended to many of the wounded, applying salves and bandages. She had many cots scattered along the walls of her dining room. She cooked and served as many as her supplies would allow. The king's men had begun making deliveries from the storehouses to her doorstep, aiding her as she aided her fair city. Margarite was a stronghold for this city, and all treated her with utter respect and gratitude. As day two was ending, Margarite found herself exhausted, having not slept for two nights. She had scurried at top speed from the moment the chaos had started. Volunteers assisting in and around the inn insisted she take rest. They would carry on the many chores still needed in this makeshift hospital.

Margarite drew some water and ascended the stairs to her keep. Her bones ached, and mentally she was exhausted. Enough was enough.

As she washed the day's grime from her body, her mind swirled with worry about Lilly. She pondered how in the world that little lass was going to manage to travel home safely. During Lilly's brief stay, Margarite had grown quite fond of her. Her playful antics and funny mannerisms were a breath of fresh and youthful air that Margarite found welcome. It had been years since she had felt that warm inner glow that comes from being motherly to the young. Margarite saw in Lilly what she had once seen in her own daughter almost a decade ago. Missing Lilly now was bringing back the same sad longing shed had tried so hard to push aside—out of viewing—away from feeling.

Nine years prior, Margarite's daughter, Sarah, had succumbed to a terrible fever during the coldest winter in decades. The same fever took many lives that year, and sadly, Sarah was one of the casualties of that horrid illness. The memory of her passing still haunted Margarite daily. She had not left her daughter's bedside for days. She and her husband tried to run the inn and monitor their little girl's illness at the same time, but it became too much for them. The doors of the inn closed as they both sat bedside holding her hand as she shivered and sweat. The worst experience of Margarite's life was when her daughter's grip of her hand eased and fell limp. Even now, all these years later, she still remembered every idiosyncrasy of those final moments with her daughter. Now, thinking of Lilly, that same gut-wrenching sorrow flooded her mind. Tonight, she was too tired to cry. She was worn too thin to give out any more emotional effort.

She settled into her covers and shut her eyes. "God Speed, little girl. God Speed."

* * *

Across town, King Lawrence was in council with his chief soldiers.

"Men, your crews have done well. The queen and I have made rounds through the city assessing damages. I'm proud of how your sentinels have supported the city. Things are coming together well for such a disaster."

The two men accepted the praise vowing to continue.

"After tomorrow, I feel that we can spare the two of you. I want you to make the journey to the meteor site. Bring me news of what you find. We will make a plan to excavate if signs show the possibility of jewels beneath that ground. I don't know what you will find, but I want a full assessment of everything from the terrain to the water flow in and out nearby. You will make this trip in secret and with haste. Three days should be more than sufficient. Return immediately. Understood?"

The men agreed and bowed to the king, taking their leave to prepare for travel.

Although the king was fascinated with precious gems, his mind was thinking financially about them also. Perhaps he could keep the finest of them, and then barter with the others to help cover expenses from the damages done during the meteor crash. Maybe the disaster that caused this mayhem could finance its repercussions. In his mind, the wheels were turning. It was exciting to consider the treasure that could come from all of this dismay. He would have answers soon.

"This could get exciting!"

28

Lilly was beside herself. These Literati, these men her mother had so warned her about, were now offering graciously to escort her home for her safety. She was humbled and thankful that men she did not know where risking life and limb to help her travel homeward.

"I don't know how to thank you. I barely know you, and you are willingly offering to take me home. I don't know what to say."

"Say that you are ready," Shark explained. "Nightfall is only a few hours away. We must make haste. We will get as far as possible until dark. We will bed down and wait until dawn. Our path is not safe at night. Even daytime may prove the same. Let's go."

Three unlikely companions stepped foot upon the Old Road, traveling north. They walked as quickly as they could, only stopping to drink at a couple small streams and splash their necks to cool down. Travel was swift for the first hour. Daniel and Lilly talked freely with one another, discussing their differences in lifestyles and future plans. It was eye-opening for them both, and it helped pass the time as they walked.

Shark walked farther ahead than the other two. His keen senses were constantly on alert—his eyes and ears scouring everything before them. Just over an hour into their journey, Shark stopped in his tracks and shushed his two followers. All stood silent as Shark took in his surroundings. He motioned for the two to stand still, and he crept forward hearing and sensing something out of place ahead.

Ahead, near the trail, Shark could tell that something or someone was either alive or dead along the side of the road. The closer he crept, the more he could hear scant breathing and a quiet moaning hum. He elected to take his chances and step closer, sword drawn and alert.

Soon, he detected a very large foot protruding from a tuft of grasses near the road. A few more steps revealed an enormous troll nestled deeply into the brush. The troll was indeed alive. His eyes stared into Shark's as he growled out a sentence.

"What are you lookin' at, Sailor?"

It was startling to see the troll almost camouflaged in the grasses. His gruff voice was piercing. Daniel and Lilly heard it as well, and it sent chills up their spine.

"Well!" shouted the troll. "Speak!"

Shark was at a loss for words. The troll's words were intimidating, yet somehow his demeanor was not as frightful as expected. Shark finally broke his silence.

"I believe I'm looking at an injured troll."

"Brilliant deduction, Sailor."

"Why are you here?"

"My business is my own." The troll grunted. "Go on! Leave me to die in peace."

Shark peered down at the troll's wounded leg. It was badly burned and bleeding. The troll tried to hide the fact that his body was trembling with fever. His hands and face had minor burns also, but the leg had severe damage.

"What is your name, troll?"

"I'm Ravok, if it was any of your business."

The wheels in Shark's head were turning, putting together pieces of this troll's puzzle.

"You … you were one of three, were you not? You were on your way to pilfer Stone Castle."

He turned his gaze away from Shark, huffing. He didn't have to answer. Shark had discerned that it was true.

"You were," stated Shark. "Why shouldn't I slay you here and now?!"

"Oh, come on, Sailor." The troll's voice trailed off. "I'm in terrible pain, the only two friends I ever had just left me to die, and the only woman I ever had a chance of loving …" The troll paused with a grimace. "… I watched her burn alive. Slay me? You pompous thug! You'd be doing me favor."

By now, Lilly and Daniel had crept close, hearing the troll's words. Neither knew if they should be feeling hatred or compassion. They stood quietly and let Shark do the talking.

"Perhaps more trolls will come to your aid."

"Not likely." Ravok continued. "All of Troll Country is burned. Maybe half of us survived and most of who did are hurt. Most are traveling north into the Dark Lands, probably to the same fate as me. And since you seem to know of my two so-called friends, I'll assume you've taken their lives. Correct?"

Shark nodded. "We had no choice. We offered them food, but they chose aggression instead. I set their bodies ablaze only hours ago."

Ravok's head shook slowly side to side. "Therein lies your answer. No one will come. Just kill me now and let me save what shred of honor I have left."

A few minutes ago, it would have been easy for Shark to thrust his sword into any troll … but now having heard the troll's plight, it seemed an incredibly difficult task. His hand twitched upon the hilt of his sword.

"Don't let me die of thirst and starvation. The pain is horrid! Do it, Sailor! End this pathetic life I lead. Do it!" Ravok grimaced as he repositioned his leg, trying not to growl as he did. He shuffled his body up and faced Shark with a scowl. "Go on, Coward!"

Just as Shark was about to unsheathe his sword, Lilly spoke up.

"Wait! Please just wait. Give me a minute." Lilly raced off of the road and into the nearby forest. Daniel and Shark gave one another questioning glances. Ravok only stared.

Soon, Lilly returned with an armload of leaves and two hands full of purple berries. She called to Daniel. "I need a cloth of some sort!"

Daniel rummaged through his satchel and found a small blanket he'd stored for sleeping.

"Cut it into full length strips." She walked straight to the leery troll and stood next to his wounded leg. She looked him in the eye. "This is going to hurt. Please trust me."

Ravok was hurting bad enough to try anything. Something about this girl settled him. Again, she looked him in the eye and let him know she was about to begin doing whatever she had planned. The troll nodded, dreading the outcome.

Lilly rubbed both her hands together with the berries in between. Once lathered, she slid both hands down the troll's wounds. Ravok let out a shriek but tried not to jerk at his leg. She then placed her green leaves side by side over all the surface of his burned skin. Daniel handed her his tattered rags. She quickly doused them with her water bottle and began wrapping his leg fully down to his toes. The physical touch of the cloth was painful, but the cool water soothed it some.

"The berries will help it heal. The leaves will help with the pain."

Shark spoke up. "We need to go. Nightfall is coming."

"Not yet," she replied. "Just a moment."

Lilly stood up beside the troll's bandaged leg and faced him again. She opened her pouch and pulled out her only loaf of bread. She tore off a third of what she had and placed it back in her pouch. She then laid both the remaining bread and her water pouch at the troll's side.

She turned quickly, trying not to get emotional. Her eyes had already started to tear up.

"My lady," the troll asked.

Lilly turned and eyed the troll once more.

Ravok spoke up. "What is your name, Little One?"

Lilly stammered. "I'm Lilly. Lilly Riverpool."

Ravok was silent for a moment, seemingly fighting some inner urge. A tear slid from his eye and down his rough cheek.

Finally, he uttered, "Thank you."

* * *

An hour later, the sun was setting in the West. The three had made good time traveling, and Shark was looking for a place to settle in for the night. Daniel and Lilly had made small talk for most of the walk, which made time pass a little quicker. Obviously, most of the trip was in a rush, but this leg of the journey was pleasant for the two to get to know one another to some degree.

"How did you know how to treat that troll's burn wounds?" asked Daniel.

"Momma showed me when I was young. We tend to most wounds in our village. It's just something that's been passed down through our generations."

"I think it's fascinating. I would like to know the names of the plants you used. I'd like to see them again, too for a visual. If it truly helps Ravok, or whatever his name was, then it was quite the blessing you gave."

"It should help him if it wasn't already too late. Sometimes, if it's been too long, Momma says the rot sets in. Sickness takes over, and it could still be deadly." Lilly's description was crude but accurate.

Daniel was taking in all she had to say. "We call it infection," he stated.

"I think I've heard it called that, too. We don't always use the fancy words." Lilly blushed.

Daniel had been watching Lilly closely as they walked, taking in her mannerisms and learning what he could of her home and village. As differently as the two lived, they still found that they had much in common, especially with their love of nature and the inquisitiveness of the unknown. It had been a learning experience for them both. Lilly had quizzed him about his lifestyle at the castle and about his hometown of Blue Haven. She hoped to visit that city one day and see the nearby ocean. She had heard tales of The Green Sea and longed to see it in all its beauty. Perhaps one day she would. She now knew she could find a guide, and it didn't hurt that he was quite handsome!

Soon, the three found a cluster of trees with low-lying limbs that could offer shelter from the dew and provide cover from outsider eyes if anyone should pass. As each settled into their places for the night, Shark filled in the two of tomorrow's plan.

"If we run into no trouble, we should make the River Pool by mid-day. I'm not certain of the precise location of the village, so I'm assuming you will be able to find a familiar path once we draw near."

"If you can find that water, I will most definitely find home! I'm so worried about what we will find. I pray they are safe. I still hold hope. Since the meteor missed the lake, the perhaps the flood will have been their only problem. All my people can swim."

"Take heart, my lady," suggested Shark, "sleep well, for you will need your rest no matter what we find. Your people are resilient. That is a comfort."

Lilly knew that Shark was right, but worry is a fear that does not have to make sense. One does not simply shut off worry.

It sleeps with you.

29

The morning sun began to shine on the southern banks of The River Pool. The village was awake at dawn, as usual, and still more cleanup was underway. Lilly's father caught himself staring toward the trail of the Snowy Pass. A hundred times a day, he'd cast a glance in that direction, almost willing the trail to produce his daughter. A thousand questions were on his mind. Had she gotten to a safe place before the explosion? Did she make it to Cobblestone? What if someone had hurt her? No, no, he couldn't think of that. She simply must be safe, and that's that. She will come, even if it's the next moon as she'd promised.

Kato had missed his big sister every bit as much as his parents. He constantly asked about when she'd return, already knowing the answer but hoping it had somehow changed since the last time he asked. He didn't just miss Lilly. He missed all the things that went along with her being near. His lessons on rock and water were nonexistent in this state of shock his village was going through. He was hungrier than usual due to the lack of time for hunting the snails which were their main food. Plus, the flood had rearranged the entire shore as they knew it.

Hunting snails would now be from scratch, digging to find new special spots in which to hunt. There were no berries and very few nuts. The village wasn't starving, but it was certainly hungrier than ever before. Now partially settled, more hunters were sent for any variety of food they could find. Kato wished he could tag along with them, just so he could pretend he was searching alongside his sister.

"Momma, I miss Lee-lee."

"I know, my sweet boy. We all do. Let's see if we can rustle up some snails."

Much to the village's surprise, the rapidly receding water had left behind food none would have expected. As the water table dropped, small puddles and pools were dammed up in places where there never had been before. Trapped inside these muddy pools were small fish! Easily caught by hand in the shallow water, the village would happily disregard their usual diet of plant-based food for fresh fish roasted over the campfires. Lilly's father said it best.

"Even in disaster, there are blessings if we choose to look for them."

* * *

The morning of day three in Cobblestone was much the same as day two. Much of the same work was being done around the city, and Cobblestone was looking better as the hours passed. There was a rush to plant late summer vegetables in the gardens that were now mostly washed away. The farmers salvaged what they could of what was left and planted anything that could grow quickly. Hunters were out in force, finding fresh meat in the way of deer, rabbits, and squirrels. The farm animals had fared through the storm well, but they, too, could be in short supply in the days to come. By and large, the city was reverting back to some sense of normalcy, and life was finding its way back into Cobblestone.

Meanwhile, the king's scouts had packed their bags and loaded their horses for travel the following morning. The king was impatient for them to leave but consoled himself with the hope that perhaps jewels would help rebuild his city.

Jewels would certainly put a smile on his face, even if no one else shared his desire for them.

30

Lilly's neck was sore from her sleeping position. The three woke with the sun and began their trek. The Old Road was quiet in the morning dew with only the sounds of birds and tree frogs chirping throughout the forest.

They'd only traveled a few minutes when a path opened to their left. Shark directed them down the path eastward. Lilly spoke up.

"Is this the Iceland Pool trail?"

"It is," answered Shark. "We should be near your home before nightfall."

Lilly perked up with that news. She was so very nervous and anxious for information. She desperately wanted to see her family. It seems worry had awoken along with her body.

By midday, they had made good travel time and the path had been vacant and quiet. At once, Shark shushed his companions and raised an ear to the sky. Through the leaves high in the trees, shadows of three birds soared overhead. Shark's eyes lit up.

"Lock! Here!" he shouted.

The birds were started by the shout but came together and soared down through the leaves toward them. It was Lock and two other Tower Ravens. The largest of the three landed on Shark's arm as he spoke.

"Lock! It is good to see you!" The bird nodded his head playfully as Shark petted his dark feathers. Some of the old bird's feathers had grayed with age, but he was still a playful and sharp old bird. As he continued to pet Lock, he called to Lilly.

"Lilly, find me a small Hemlock branch. They only grow here along this trail. Elias will know we've made it this far. Make sure it has its tiny cones still attached."

Lilly did as she was told and fetched a small branch. She asked, "Why the cones on the branch?"

"Cones are a sign of plenty. It means we are doing well. An empty branch means we are in danger."

Both Lilly and Daniel were astounded by Shark's knowledge of the secret messages that the Literati had created via Tower Ravens. There were countless other hidden messages in the smallest of things that ravens could carry along in flight. It was a system that evolved over decades, and its benefits grew along with its implementation.

The Tower Ravens originated from the lineage of ravens that resided in and around the rocky bluffs that overlooked The Green Sea north of The Bay of Greenwale. The section of forest was known as Ravenclutch. This high and rocky terrain was part of the Iceland Mountains where rock met sea and the North Fork River emptied. Enormous Cedar trees clung to the bluff walls and the ancient and twisted Black Pines cradled raven's nests in their boughs. In times of great need, when stores of food were low on the sailing ships, sailors would go ashore and rob nests of eggs for food. It was a dangerous business climbing high above the sea from limb to limb, so it was only in times of great need that travelers would risk life and limb to eat. Plus, the ravens could put up quite a battle defending their nests.

It was during one of these desperate times that a large batch of raven eggs were collected and brought back to the ship. Before the eggs were eaten, the ship had taken harbor at The Bay of Greenwale. There, the eggs were traded for other goods and fell into the hands of a young student at a monastery near town. Being the keeper of chickens at this large church, he instinctively placed the eggs under one of his setting hens. In a matter of weeks, he soon was in possession of ten baby ravens. Naturally, the mother hen shunned the babies, so the young man nurtured these tiny creatures, feeding them and talking to them like a mother. Seven of the original ten survived and flourished.

This raven parent boy was named Eldon, but the townspeople called him Bird Boy. Everywhere he went, seven feathery companions flew nearby. The city folk were amazed at his communication with his pets. Not only did the birds understand many things the boy said, but he, too, knew their coos and caws and head posture. It was comical to watch him talk with his birds. Each sentence was animated with head bobbing, arms and wings flapping in a certain way. People would gather around to watch the spectacle. They would roar with appreciation when a raven would speak a few words and answer real questions with a 'yes' or 'no'.

Soon, those ravens hatched still more babies. Within two years, this young peasant boy had become quite wealthy selling off a few of his flock. It was then that the true treasure of these birds became known.

The Steward of the nearby city of Blue Haven purchased three pairs of ravens for an enormous amount of money. He moved them high into the city's castle tower, and there he treated them like royalty. He had kept them penned for nearly a year until young birds were hatched and started to grow. He then set free one of the pairs of birds to see if they would remain nearby their new home.

Much to the Steward's dismay, the pair flew away immediately. Two days passed without sign of their beautiful black feathers. And then it happened. On the eve of the second day, both birds returned and lit on the precipice ledge, almost smiling. One of the birds had a note attached to its leg. He quickly untied the note and read it. It was from Eldon! He was able to tell the birds to return home, assuring them that they could visit again at any time.

Thusly, the Tower Raven system of message travel was born. Soon, Cobblestone would acquire birds. Learned men from other parts of Greenwale would purchase them, too. The man known as Tolk carried his bird along with him at all times, making his way from castle to castle and even deep into the forests. These birds were much more than friendly pets. These were highly intelligent companions. They were remarkable messengers. They were life-long beloved family members. Their value was beyond measure.

After the ravens were sent back to Stone Castle, the three continued their march eastward. The hours passed quickly for Daniel and Lilly. They had covered many topics and shared much of their hopes and dreams. They had developed a strong bond, despite being raised in to two very different homes. They still made minor jousts toward one another, poking fun at their differences, but a common respect had been born.

"By my calculations," Shark said, "the pool should be ahead, just over this ridge."

In minutes, the three stood overlooking the beautiful, but muddy, Iceland Pool. Lilly's heart soared as she calculated where they stood versus the proximity of her village.

Shark commented, "It think its farther east."

Lilly's head turned side to side. "YES! I know where we are!"

Without thinking of her companions, she bolted into a run toward home, only thinking of her family and how fast she could run.

"Should we keep up or give her some space before we get there?" Daniel asked.

"Nothing is chasing us. If you think I'm running, you're mistaken."

31

As the afternoon sun was settling behind the trees of The Deep Forest, Stone Castle was now in council. News from the Tower Ravens was comforting, and now the Literati were in debate over the last writings and words of Tolk. Eighteen-year-old Claybon, Daniel's friend, had a reasonable question to ask.

"What is Myrtos, and how are we to nurture it?"

Most of the Literati had already discerned part of what Claybon had asked. The first lesson for new Literati alumni is to learn the Greek language. The lessons that followed all hinged upon first learning that foreign language. Much of what was studied at the castle was documented in Greek.

Elias addressed the question aloud for all to ponder.

"Myrtos is Greek for Myrtle, a vinelike plant that grows over the ground and climbs its way up tree trunks. It blooms beautiful blue flowers. And before you ask, Master Claybon, Myrtos rarely needs tending. It chokes out many other varieties of plants and takes over sections of the woods. Why we need to nurture it is why we've gathered. Tolk's words baffle me."

It was a perplexing question that no one there could answer.

The topic of the Shard came up next. Some of the Elders had already scoured numerous books where certain jewels were mentioned, but none found answers matching Tolk's suggestions. All present assumed that these two questions most definitely pertained to the meteor crash, but none could make sense of how the two questions corresponded with one another.

"It seems we are at a standstill," remarked Elias. "Two of our volunteers are currently on another mission. I expect their return late tomorrow. The ravens have brought a tell-tale sign back from near the Iceland Pool. The Hemlock branch with cones offers the likelihood that the group is safe. My suggestion for this council is to wait for their return. Then, we send them on the next journey to evaluate the meteor site. Perhaps they will find the answers we seek."

Elias paused for the council to ponder his suggestion. He then offered more information.

"We have been studying the last scribes of Tolk. They, too, are quite vague. The Elders will be holding a separate council to attempt to decipher his words and illustrations. Until then, we must still man our posts for intrusion. The rest of you should try to get back to your studies and pray that some sense of normalcy shall return."

The meeting adjourned as the crowd discussed this day's topic. All had the same bewilderment.

"How do we nurture Myrtle?"

* * *

Two Cobblestone sentinels were packed and ready for the ride tomorrow. The king was pleased with the progress in town and now focused on what could be found at the meteor site. He'd have to wait another couple of days for his answers, but he was inspired that the news would soon be brought to him.

He thought to himself, "I wonder if the Literati will be going there, too?"

32

Lilly's muddy feet raced as fast as they would carry her. She crested the final hill before descending into the valley and out onto the shoreline. Ahead, she could see her villagers scattered about her home. Someone spotted her and began to yell to the others. The entire village emptied in her direction with young Kato at the head of the pack.

Seconds later, Kato jumped headlong into Lilly's chest and grabbed hold, toppling her backward onto the ground. Tears of joy poured from their eyes, and they squeezed tighter than ever before. She managed to stand with the lad still holding onto her for dear life. Her parents raced to her side, also pulling her into a giant family hug. Such happiness and relief filled their hearts just knowing that their baby girl was home safe. The villagers roared with cheers of happiness. At least for the moment, the weight of worry over the meteor damage was lifted. All rejoiced in the precious homecoming.

In the distance, Daniel and Shark followed Lilly's footprints in the mud and soon entered into the village. The townspeople welcomed them to the best of their ability, having never done such a thing before.

Their usual mode with other walks of life was to hide. If any intruder lingered too long, one of the Wild Folk would come forward for discussion. If there was any altercation that ensued, an entire village of angry Wild Folk would emerge will bamboo sticks whirling. No one would dare challenge this band of people. They were every bit as formidable as tales of old. So, with a new perspective, the village folk welcomed the men and thanked them many times over for their immense help. It was exciting for all during this strange and chance encounter.

As evening darkness was covering the land, the villagers gathered around the campfire to hear about Lilly's adventures. Shark and Daniel were near, as well, and offered other news from around Greenwale. The Wild Folk were amazed at Lilly's travels and tales of Trolls and of the wonderful food Margarite had introduced her to. She raved and raved about Margarite's breads and rolls, as well as that of the Literati. Their cheeses made the top of her list, also. There was just so much to share, it seemed she could not tell it all. Such wonder! Such danger! So much life she had known nothing about. "Momma, it was the most amazing week of my life!"

And Lilly meant it.

She was told of the night of the meteor and of how they narrowly escaped its wrath. She heard about the flood and about how monstrously fast the waters had risen. She was informed of the clean up and salvage of the village, which was still in progress and would be for some time to come.

Shark and Daniel informed the crowd that they would be taking leave at daybreak to carry news back to the Literati. They had been fed well by the villagers—foods that they had never eaten. Getting past the thought of eating a snail right out of the shell was difficult, but once that delicacy was pulled from the fire and offered them, their hunger took over, and they ate their fill. Surprisingly, both found the taste of snail to be quite good. With a few raw vegetables and nuts, they were very satisfied. Soon, they found a comfortable place to nestle in for the night and dozed off to sleep.

Lilly kept telling details of her travels well into late evening. Her stories seemed impossible to her family and friends. Her mother just couldn't believe that her little girl had experienced so many things, and she could tell that what she had witnessed had changed her in many ways. She was still Daddy's little girl, but that little girl was far more worldly now than just a mere week before. Lilly had gotten a taste of the world, and she was not about to settle for anything less than grand ever again. She had decided that the good was worth the bad out there in the bigness of it all.

And in her mind, she was already planning more trips.

33

Shark and Daniel were well on their way before dawn's first light. A few hours into their travel, Daniel finally asked the question that was on both of their minds.

"What are we going to do with the troll?"

Shark had very few ideas. He only grunted. "Ugh. I don't know."

Both men were pondering if they could somehow transport him elsewhere, perhaps to a food and water source. That solution was not pragmatic. Where would that place be? No doubt, the Literati would have no part in him. Perhaps they could give him what little food and water they had left and leave him to heal or die trying. Neither sounded plausible.

As they came upon the site of the troll, both stood bewildered.

The troll was gone.

"Well, now," huffed Shark. "It seems our problem has solved itself."

Soon the men entered Stone Castle. They were quizzed for details of their trip and advised to restock for the next journey as they spoke. It was a whirlwind as they scurried to ready themselves for the trip. They received instruction from Elias as they packed their satchels. They were to leave immediately and return as quickly as they came once they had secured details from the site. With little to go on, they suited up and dashed out the door once more. This time, Claybon tagged along for good measure. He was considerably more intrigued with the trip than the other two simply because he had not been on the last ragged trip through the forest trails.

Judging by the sound of the meteor crash and red glow of the forest fires of that night, they elected to travel almost due west in hopes of centering the meteor's location.

* * *

The king's men sped into the forest on horseback, making their way northeastward. The took the same path that Lilly had been searching for on her initial trip to Cobblestone. The trail led from their city northward and would later branch off to the east about forty miles into the journey. They had been underway since dawn, and the horses had covered much ground before midday.

As the two sentinels reached the northward Snowy Pass, they veered left onto it and started their ascent. Soon, they came across the dead and bloated body of a Snow Troll along the trail. Neither had ever seen a Snow Troll before, so they took a moment to take a visual. The huge beast was every bit as terrifying as its reputation, with its long whitish hair and sharp fangs and claws. Its lower leg was badly injured, and it had bled profusely over the ground where the troll lay. The beast had evidently bled to death from its wounds. Judging by the rotten stench, this must have happened close to a week before. The decay was a nasty sight.

They continued upward on the trail farther toward the top. It wasn't long before the trail came to an abrupt end. A muddy and charred ravine had cut a gouge through the trail. Obviously, it was the meteor's path of destruction.

The two were forced to double back down the mountain, past the dead troll, and reconnect with their original path. Their travel had slowed once they had rejoined that path due to overgrown briars and trees in their way. This part of the forest was rarely traveled, and it proved more difficult to navigate. Still, they pressed on, seeing and sensing signs of destruction. Ash and mud were all about them, and many trees were merely charred and burned stumps. The forest had changed since the two had traveled here. The ground had changed elevation here and there, and it was difficult to tell if this trail would still exist father ahead. What was once a valley cut with streams now showed signs of higher elevation. The meteor had pushed soil upward, changing the landscape considerably.

It was obvious to the men that they were very close to the crash site, although this pile of soil in front of them was foreign. Their horses edged up the hillside and peered over the top. As the horses crested the hill and stood on top, both men sat in awe at what they saw. Between the meteor crash and the torrential rain, a small lake had been formed. As the meteor exploded into the ground, it ejected rock and mud out of the ground, creating a crater in the center of the woods. The debris landed all around and created a dam. As the heavy rains fell, it filled this crater with water. The upper stream had changed course and now created a wondrous waterfall on its upper eastward side. It flowed overtop the cavern created by the meteor burning its way into the earth. A cave was formed beneath the waterfall, hidden from eyesight. The men had no doubts that the cave was the final resting spot of the meteor. They needed only to enter to see what the underground looked like in comparison to the lay of the ground outside.

They wasted no time dismounting their horses. It was difficult to maneuver the outside terrain of the cave. Rocks and burned logs were scattered about the slippery mud. A path could easily be carved along the water's edge once any plans were made to mine the cave if the king should wish to do so.

The water was cold and still muddy from the rains. The two men took a deep breath and splashed through the waterfall and into the cave tunnel behind. Although it was quite dark inside, enough sunlight shone through the waterfall to catch a glimpse of the meteor's burrowing path into the ground. Along the dark tunnel walls, sparkles could be seen reflecting from its surface. Indeed, there were jewels left behind from the meteor's burning pressure as it melted its way down into the earth. It was the information they needed for the king.

The men returned back through the waterfall entrance. After a visual of the lay of the land outside the tunnel, the two mounted their horses and galloped away toward Cobblestone.

The king would be quite pleased.

* * *

The morning after the king's men had left the meteor site, three other visitors walked into the devastation caused by the meteor. Shark, Daniel, and Claybon viewed this large body of water that had not been here only days before. The waterfall was gloriously pretty, and the plants and trees nearby seemed to be greening up faster than ordinary. The ground was still scorched and muddy, but small plants were just beginning to sprout over the ground surface. The men were amazed at how quickly Mother Nature could begin to reclaim her forest. It'd only been a few days, but the landscape appeared as if it was longer than that.

They, too, surmised that the waterfall housed the meteor's entry into the ground. Soon, they, too, would be inside staring at the sparkling walls of the cave. None had expected to find jewels in this array of carnage. If the Literati had suspected this, they had not shared it with the three men now witnessing them.

With no form of light to investigate further, the three left the cave and sat upon a boulder just outside. They sat quiet for a few moments, filling their flasks with water and taking in the sounds of nature. It was Shark to first speak up.

"Something seems strange about this place—remarkable, actually. Even in this mess, the forest seems very much alive to me. Do you feel it?"

Both other men had already came to that same conclusion but had not shared their thoughts yet. Daniel gave his thoughts.

"I can't put my finger on it, but there is something about this area that feels vibrant. I expected to feel differently when we arrived. Sad, maybe. Shocked? I don't know what it is, but I feel it."

Claybon agreed and gave his assessment. "I know the sound of every bird in the forest. I've heard a different sound—a cooing sound like a Mourning Dove, only shorter. That noise is foreign to me."

Shark and Daniel had not expected such a reply from Claybon. Neither knew that Claybon was quite the bird fancier. Both were impressed and quizzed him for further description.

"I noticed before we arrived by the water. It wasn't just one sound from one direction. There were many similar ones in all directions. Whatever birds made this sound, they were surrounding us. I think they were watching us—at least that is what I felt."

By now, Shark and Daniel had begun listening, too. They could hear what Claybon was talking about. The sound was ever so quiet, almost distant. At times it was harmonious, as if two or more were chirping together.

And then there were these rapidly growing young saplings popping up in the mud and ash. What could make a forest regrow so quickly?

Realizing they had no answers to their questions, the began their trek back to Stone Castle. If they hurried, they could make it by midday tomorrow. Claybon was rather enjoying his travels, but the other two were long since ready for a comfortable bed. Daniel couldn't wait to remove his boots and soak them in warm water. Shark, too, desperately wanted to bathe and rest his feet. The sooner they got started, the sooner they could attain all those things.

It was time to travel east.

34

The Literati Elders had been in a private group studying the writings of Tolk. His prophesies were indeed vague and confusing, but bits and pieces were slowly falling into place.

Elias shared a page he had been pondering.

"I think I might have something here. Let me read you an excerpt. *From fiery night it fell as if from burning Hell. It scorched into the ground to places still unfound. And from disaster came life without a name. They pulled their roots from land and walked on foot and hand. And raised by human fist came the Shard of Amethyst.*"

All agreed that these quatrains definitely were about the meteor. Plants walking made no sense at all to any of them. Both these quatrains and Tolks last words mentioned a shard, but amethyst was not registering as anything familiar.

Elias kept reading. "*Trust in she, trust in she, for without her, they shall not be … Myrtos!*"

"There it is again," spoke Nathaniel. "Myrtos. The thing we must nurture."

"It's getting late, men," spoke Elias. "Let us adjourn and give it more thought. Perhaps our team will return tomorrow with answers."

It seemed that the more they studied, the more questions they had. Now, they had a new question—one far more vague than any other.

"Who in the world is *SHE*?"

35

As the next two weeks unfolded, the King Marcus was making his plans for excavating jewels from the meteor site. Cobblestone was still under cleanup, and the townspeople were coping with the aftermath of what had transpired.

Margarite had resumed business at the inn, and those she had cared for had moved on from her establishment to start rebuilding their lives. Lilly crossed her mind often, and she wondered if she'd ever see the little lass ever again. She reflected on the days she'd spent with her, remembering her playful antics and love of life.

Stone Castle had been quiet, with no troll encounters after the first sad intrusion. Perhaps the trolls had moved north as Ravok had stated. The Elders had continued to ponder Tolk's writings, finally deciding that some other upcoming occurrence would shed some light for them. Communications via the Tower Ravens was scant. Neither the Literati, nor Cobblestone Castle, were willing to share their plans for their trip to the meteor site, hoping secrecy would allow each to investigate without intrusion from the other. Jewels really weren't in the Literati's mindset, but Tolk's writings were weighing heavily upon their minds.

Lilly's village was getting back to normal. The Wild Folk had no buildings to repair, and most of their surroundings were fairly easy to refabricate. New snail habitats were found, and food was now more abundant since the lake elevation had fallen to usual levels. The incoming streams had flushed most of the Iceland Pool of debris, and even the North Fork River was calming also. The river had changed course in more than one spot, but the woodland creatures had returned to their grounds to live as before.

On this particular morning, Lilly and Kato were hunting snails along the water's edge east of their camp. As the dew was drying along shore, Lilly caught the familiar sound of the water harp in the distance. She smiled as usual at the sound, enjoying the morning with Kato. The sweet voice that always accompanied the water harp was drifting along with the water currents as they sifted the silt for snails. She had lost herself in the music when Kato posed a question.

"Its beautiful, don't you think?"

"I'm sorry, Kato. I was lost in thought. What's beautiful?"

"I thought you heard it, too," he said. "Her water harp is the nicest sound in the world. She's wonderful!"

Lilly was beside herself. She had thought that she was the only one on Earth that could hear voices and music in the water. The fact that Kato named the sound *she* really surprised her.

"Kato, did you say SHE?"

"Of course, Leelee. You know her, right?"

"Tell me more, Kato. What have you seen?"

"Oh, I don't have to tell. You'll see!"

In her talk with Kato, she had not realized that the sounds that she was hearing were growing louder and evidently closer. She gazed out over the pool, almost expecting to see something ... something water-ish.

Kato sat down on the shoreline and crossed his arms over his legs. He closed his eyes as a warm smile pulled at his cheeks. Lilly took note and sat down alongside him and did the same. She found that when she closed her eyes and really listened, that the voice seemed clearer and the water harp even more pure. Both sat peacefully, simply enjoying the moment.

With eyes still closed, Kato whispered to Lilly.

"It won't be long now."

Lilly barely heard his words. She was lost somewhere between her head and her heart, letting the music and lyrics sooth her soul. The music's delicate, tender, succulent drippings of purity encompassed everything within ear's distance. It was as if the heavens had rained down blessings and love.

Amid this haze of grandeur, the voice was still heard, whispering love and happiness as it flowed. It was a sleepless dream of beauty, all encompassing.

Lilly let her eyes open just a little to take in the sights as well as the sound. In seconds, her eyes were wide open, and she sprang to her feet in awe.

"OH, MY!"

Before them both was a being like nothing they had ever witnessed. Amid the swirling currents of the water, the form of a woman emerged. Her shape seemed to be formed of water … ever flowing back into the pool. When she wished, her shape would take on color and depth, reflecting the nature around her, and then wash away again into the falling water. She appeared to be part of her surroundings … and yet somehow creating it at the same time. The sounds of water filled their ears. Cool, humid air comforted them both as they wept in the splendor of the being before them.

And behold … the being spoke.

"Welcome, Little Ones! I have waited long for this day! Come with me and rejoice in my waters. Rejoice in my life—in my love."

Her face flushed with warm hues, and her lips smiled with contentment.

At that moment, the being began to stroke the dripping cords of an enormous golden water harp that also washed up to her beckoning hands, somehow rushing from the depths of the pool and filling her wondrous hands. Harmony filled the air … notes blended seamlessly with the sounds of the forest. The two were swept away into her presence and into the currents of voices and notes and the beautiful, quiet whisperings of nature. They were speechless as they stared in wonder.

"All is well, my friends," spoke the voice again. "Join me. Rejoice with me in my waters."

Lilly could barely speak. Her eyes were hopelessly drawn to the beauty before her. "Not—not in all my teachings … have I heard of such a being. Never have I known such beauty. Who … who are you?"

"I will take that as a compliment, young Lilly Riverpool." Her face flushed with almost human-like colors when she spoke, and her smile radiated when the siblings spoke. "And young Kato…have you forgotten how to speak?"

Lilly desperately wanted to ask how she knew their names but couldn't utter a word. She simply gazed into her eyes, being completely engulfed in the moment and melted by her presence.

Kato finally uttered a few words. "I felt you before. Who are you?"

The woman raised her flowing hands from the harp and reached toward them. She picked them from the shoreline and placed them on her lap, as the water flowed around them. With her face flushing in wonderful hues, she spoke again.

"Young ones…you do not know my name, but you have always known me. You have swam in my pools … floated in my currents. You have given me great pleasure. I have cradled you in my waters, loving your spirit, embracing your love of life."

She smiled warmly as her face beamed with color and emotion. "Little ones … I am Aquavita! I am the Spirit of Water! I am the driving force—the rejuvenating pureness to the waters of the world. I have come to you now for your task is at hand. It is time for you to play your parts. I come bearing news for you."

"News…?" mumbled Lilly, feeling lightheaded.

"You, little ones, will be famed beyond that of your kin. You…" she smiled, "…will shape the fate of the forest."

They had no more words. The sheer grandeur of Aquavita was too captivating. They were awestruck trying to understand her sweet words.

Aquavita chuckled softly at their state of mind, her body flowing in shades of blue and green. She picked them up again, still smiling all aglow.

"Wake up, siblings! You have a journey to make."

"What?" Lilly chirped, shaking water from her brow. She spoke up again. "We know nothing of what you speak. We know nothing beyond our tiny section of the woods. Our little bodies cannot shape forests! We are not warriors."

Aquavita beamed with joyous colors as her voice chuckled in harmonious tones. "The forest does not need warriors. It needs your hearts. You will both play a part in a grand adventure!"

All Kato could do was smile. He had no idea what was going on other than that he finally got to see the being that so often sang to him so sweetly.

Aquavita spoke again. "Lilly, you are special. The time is now for you to play your part. You must go to the meteor site—you—and you, alone. You will know when the time is right to return home. You will also know when it is time for Kato to play his part. It will encompass your whole family. It will also involve others. Your actions will affect other actions. Acquaintances will be strongholds. Friends will become dear."

Aquavita placed the two back on shore with a tender smile. Her harp once again magically arose from the pool and she began to strum its chords. As she plucked the wondrous watery notes, her body slowly slid away and melted into the waters from whence she came. On the air, her words drifted over the water. "You must go soon, Lilly. It is time for you to be you."

Her song grew quieter as she drifted away, and the waters of the Iceland Pool calmed. Lilly and Kato looked to one another with such wonder. Kato chuckled out loud.

"I getta tell Momma!" and off he ran, leaving Lilly reeling from it all.

36

Lilly's parents could barely understand Kato's excited chattering about Aquavita. By the time Lilly arrived back home, Kato had rambled endlessly about the wonders of what they'd seen. Her parents looked to Lilly for answers.

"Momma, Poppa ... it's like he says. She's real ... so very real." The glow on her face told the story. Describing who or what Aquavita was had proved difficult. Telling of such euphoria falls utterly short of the eyewitness account.

"Poppa," she continued, "you told me about Kato during the flood, and how he had told you that the water had spoken to him that *it was so*. It was her, Pappa. It was Aquavita ... the Spirit of the Water. She was so very beautiful."

Lilly's parents were speechless. It would have been easier to discount the story if it hadn't been for both siblings recounting the same tale in detail. As hard as it was to believe, they placed their trust in their children and chose to hear Aquavita's message. "What would she have us do?"

"That's just it, Pappa. The first leg of this adventure is only for me ..."

* * *

News had spread through the village in minutes. Lilly was going on another adventure, and she was going alone! She'd only just returned to them, and now she was tarrying off again. How could she toy with their hearts in such a way? From the outside looking in, Lilly's actions seemed childish and immature, but in her heart, Lilly was more certain about this than any other decision she'd ever made. If fact, she took no time to decide. For her, it was a given from the moment Aquavita spoke. She had told Lilly that it was time for her to play her part. She didn't know what that part was, but she was unquestionably certain that this was in some way her destiny.

By nightfall, she was packed and ready for first light to travel. Sleeping was to no avail. She was wound up inside and simply could not wait to see the first rays of sun come morning.

The sun finally rose. Lilly had said her good-byes the night before, and she found it easier than her previous departure. Her last trip was filled with uncertainty, carrying with her the underlying fear of the unknown. Although she knew little of her destiny, there was a certain comfort knowing that Aquavita had sent her onward—onward to fulfill her part in some grand story she nothing about. It was mysterious and exciting. It was exhilarating. Although she hadn't slept much at all, she was full of energy, and her feet were light on the trial. She was on a mission.

She had chosen to take the Snowy Pass. Shark had shown her a trail leading off the Old Road when they passed on their way to her home. He had told her that it led through the center of the woods. She had no way of knowing if back-tracking toward Stone Castle and veering west would be better or worse than taking the Snowy Pass and eventually branching off eastward. She'd encountered a troll on both paths, so ruling out either trail due to trolls wasn't a viable factor. She simply had a gut feeling about the Snowy Pass and chose it.

Midday had brought her through the Snowy Pass and a measurable distance down the mountainside. She had paid particularly close attention to the possible presence of Snow Trolls. Thankfully, she had seen nothing of the sort. The only animals she had seen were squirrels, rabbits, and a few birds. The rest of her travels were quiet.

Lilly crested a small ridge and looked down the trail. She was more than surprised to find that the trail had come to a halt. A twenty-feet wide gulley had been scraped and scorched down through the hillside. It was unquestionably the path of the meteor careening down the mountainside. Its disturbed soil was fairly fresh, and the remains of forest fires were evident of such destruction. She would either have to follow the trench or try to find a way to slide down into it, and then shimmy back up the far side back onto the trail.

The trench was definitely the correct answer. Its trajectory would lead precisely to the meteor's end.

The going was rough on that steep slope of mud, rock and ash. She longed for a better trail but kept on with the mental fortitude that she was on the right track.

She paused a few minutes into her hike down the ravine. A terrible smell was coming from the westward side. Unpleasant as it was, she felt the need to investigate where the stench was coming from.

She found a place in the ravine to climb its edge. She hoisted herself up onto flat ground and looked around. She took a few steps westward toward the Snowy Pass Trail that paralleled the meteor's ravine. It didn't take long to find the source of the smell. The three-week-old decaying carcass of a Snow Troll lie along the road. Wild animals had devoured much of the body, and the rest had been pilfered by vultures. It was a sickening sight. She knew in an instant that this was the troll that had attacked her.

Peering at the troll's leg, it was evident that the knee Lilly had struck with her sharpened bamboo was the cause of death. Tendons were severed at the kneecap. The blackish ground beneath indicated that the troll had bled to death from the wound and could not have moved without muscles attached to his lower leg. He had fallen where she'd hit him. In her heart, she knew that it had been her that killed him, and it was a slow and painful death. As wretched as the beast was, and as purely evil were his actions, it still tore at Lilly's heart. She had taken a living, breathing, speaking life. Her tender heart melted, and a tear slid down her nose. She wished she had not investigated the smell in the first place. It would have been easier never knowing the result of her actions. With a shake of her head, she crept down into the ravine and followed it downward.

She tried to remember her travels through this hillside and valley only weeks ago. Even if she could have recalled the scenery, it was doubtful it would make any difference in her navigation. She had the big path in front of her now—an enormous gouge in the land providing a telltale path for her travel.

The going was rough. Stones and soil had been pushed around into precarious areas making footing difficult. Still, she pressed on, light in spirit but wary of the countryside. Aquavita had been vague in her description of this adventure, so Lilly remained alert, taking in her surroundings as she plodded along.

The sun was trying to set as the ground beneath her began to flatten. She had taken notice that the farther downhill she had come, the greener the forest seemed. She would no doubt be coming upon the crash site soon, and it seemed strange that foliage had begun to regrow faster near the meteor site than further up the mountain where carnage was not as horrific. She walked further, searching for a place to bed down for the night. Before a suitable place was found, her journey came to an end. There it was. A large crater in the ground was filled with water, and a jumble of rocky ledges had been pushed up from the soil. The meteor had created a serious change in the structure of this valley. She had remembered crossing a large creek in her previous travels through this forest, but this gorgeous lake must certainly be new.

Above this placid pool, where the boulders had been pushed, water now poured over the top creating a wondrous waterfall. It was quite a lot to take in. Here, in this place where disaster had befallen the valley, a Utopia of water and foliage was now coming to life. Plants grew from ashes. Charred trees were starting to grow new leaves. Birds chirped. Squirrels barked. Frogs croaked. It was as if Mother Nature had kissed this special spot. What a wonder to behold!

Lilly found a pleasant overlook of the waterfall and settled in. She hadn't eaten all day and was now starved. She dug some berries and nuts from her pouch and ate as she gazed in all directions. The sights and sounds of the area eased her worries. With nightfall coming quickly, she was ready for a good night's sleep.

As she nestled into a comfortable spot, her mind turned to Aquavita's words the day before. Her young head was full of wonder, and her heart was glad.

Her eyes were growing heavy when she heard the first of many noises she'd never heard in the forest before. It was a call of some sort from an animal she knew nothing about. It was a very faint coo, calming and pure. Soon, there was another, as if in reply. Then, still more of the sounds filled the woods. There were different pitches in each sound. Some shrill, and others deeper, almost a rumble. Within minutes, the forest was in harmony with hundreds of ooos and coos, rumbles and cackles.

She felt no fear, despite the volume of sounds around her. They were peaceful calls, pleasant in nature. It was the perfect spot for this young lady to lay her head.

Tomorrow would be special. She could feel it.

37

The Literati was glad to see the three companions return from the meteor site. The three held an open forum of questions and answers. They gave account of the new crater pool and how the stream had changed course over the newly situated rocks, creating a beautiful waterfall. They told of the cave entrance behind the falls and of how the rock walls sparkled in the darkness of the cave.

The Elders were intrigued by the sparkling stones of the tunnel. They had questions about the size and colors of the stones along the walls. The men hadn't taken time to get that thorough in their investigation. They had no way of creating more light within the cave and felt rushed to bring back news of it all to Stone Castle.

The three then mentioned the rapidly regrowing plants in the area of the site. From new saplings, to fresh leaves on existing trees, the forest was awakening from the disaster. This perplexed the Elders. Burned forests take a very long time to regrow. The soil compositions change with the ash, and seeds burn before taking root. With unbalanced nutrients being the only sustenance for growth, the forest lies dormant for months, even years. This bit of information gave the Elders hope in helping decipher the writings of Tolk.

"There are new sounds as well," commented Claybon. "I am quite knowledgeable when it comes to birdsong. I know variations of different tree frog chirps. What were heard in and around the site were none of those animals. Something foreign has taken up residence there. Whatever they are, coo like a dove in the distance, ever so quiet. Some sound deeper than those of doves, while others are more like the Mountain Lark. I've never heard anything like it. It's new to me."

Although the news from their trip was simple in nature, it certainly posed many more questions. Shark could sense that the Literati wanted more information, and he could foresee another trip into the forest. He spoke up before the suggestion was made.

"We will return after the Elders have given this thought. We need rest for a few days before that happens. We have covered many miles. I, too, would like more information. We need the proper questions from the Elders before we can go search for answers."

Shark was right. Another immediate trip would not likely be useful without an investigative plan to follow once they arrived. All came to an agreement, and the meeting adjourned. The three men enjoyed a hearty meal, soaking their sore feet as they ate. Wheels were turning in every mind in the castle.

If *thinking* could solve a problem, this place would score with extra credit.

38

Lilly woke with a start. A small limb had fallen from above and landed in her lap. As she focused her sleepy eyes, she brushed the limb off her body. To her surprise, the limb rolled right back up again into her lap.

She shook her head, as if still dreaming. She brushed it off again.

Sure enough, the limb rolled right back up again into her lap! Now, she was fully awake and questioning what she had just witnessed.

Oddly, this leafy little limb seemed to move itself. As she stared closely, the smaller limbs attached to the trunk stem began to raise and lower like arms. Above those armlike limbs, rested a head of sorts.

The head had eyes!

Lilly's eyes, too, were now wide. The head of this creature was tilting back and forth, its facial expressions changing as it investigated her. At times, its eyes squinted, as if in deep thought. Then, the face would relax and almost smile. Periodically, a quiet cool would come from the creature, much like a young puppy whimpers for attention. It was as if the creature was thinking, "Awe, what a cute little animal."

The two were clearly intrigued with one another. Lilly found herself wanting to touch the creature—pet his leafy coverings. Oddly, the creature felt the same about Lilly. Her long, dark, curly hair fascinated it. It crept closer up her chest, its head tilting sideways and cooing. Its long, tentacle-like fingers reached into her hair and slid through it. It was soft to the touch. Dried flowers woven into it had a special beauty that the creature appreciated. His cooing grew louder as he stroked her hair and smiled.

Lilly couldn't resist. She slowly reached her hand toward the creature, careful of where she put her fingers. Perhaps this thing bites? She didn't ponder biting long. The solemn nature of this thing gave a certain comfort to her. She wasn't scared, and the creature appeared to evoke a sense of calm. In fact, its quiet coos and crooked little smile were so playfully cute, that Lilly wanted to hold and pet it like a kitten.

Her hand came gently near the creature's arm. It was a little standoffish but allowed the intrusion. The greenery of its arms and head felt very much leaflike. In fact, they were leaves. Dozens of them covered its body. Also, its arms, legs, and main torso looked like bark, but at the touch, it was actually quite soft and furry. It was an optical illusion. What looked like rough and crumbly bark was quite flexible and plush.

So, there they were, two odd beings petting one another in the heart of the Deep Forest.

It startled the creature when Lilly spoke.

"Well, now. Aren't you the curious one?"

The creature's head tilted side to side, its rough little eyebrows moving along with his thoughts. "Mmmmmm," it cooed. It bounced in place and smiled.

"What is it?" she asked. "You want to play? Is that it?"

The creature quickly scampered up her arm and under her hair, squirreling around her neck and down her other arm. It stopped in her lap and did a back flip.

"My, my, you're a clever one!"

"My, my," it replied.

"What? You talk?"

"My, my." It repeated.

"Oh, wow! You're … you're quite intelligent." She smiled and rubbed his leafy head. "And cute!"

"Cute!" it mimicked. "Ooooo."

Lilly was flabbergasted. "Whatever you are, you are very smart. Where did you come from? Are you a plant or an animal?"

The creature only tilted its head inquisitively.

"Hmmm," Lilly pondered. "Let walk around a bit. See what it is that you do."

As she stood, the creature shimmied up her arm and onto her shoulder, cooing and rubbing his face against her soft hair. He seemed quite content just having a new pal to share his day. She continued to speak to him as if he understood as they walked around this beautiful new pool of water. The sun was on the rise, and its rays reflected from the water like a mirror. The only ripples on the water were from the waterfall emptying from above.

She walked along the shore of the pool and peered into its surface. "Look," she said. "You can see yourself in the water. It's a mirror."

The creature looked from her shoulder down into the water. He smiled and gave a wave to his reflection. He did it several times, not understanding yet what he was seeing.

"You're clever," she said. "I wish I knew what you are. Do you have a name?"

The creature only cocked his head questioningly.

"Are you a boy or a girl? I can't tell."

Clearly, the questions were to no avail. It didn't bother the creature though. He would climb down from her now and then and scamper about, doing cartwheels and jumping from hand to foot. The creature didn't seem to have a care in the world, playing with his new friend and happily bouncing here and there.

"Well," she continued, "You act like a boy, if you ask me. Plus, you need a name. I think I'll call you Clever. That sounds fitting. And while we're at it, we need a name for what you are. You're leafy, and you act … well … youthful. Let's call you a … hmmm … a Leafling. What do you think of that?"

The Leafling only nodded as if he understood. She decided to try to teach him some new words. He'd picked up on some other words quickly.

She pointed toward him. "Clever." The Leafling nodded. She pointed to herself. "Lilly." She repeated her actions and words a few more times. "Clever."

The Leafling attempted it. "Keffer."

"You almost have it! Clever."

"Keffer. Keffer. Keffer, Keffer, Keffer! Cooo!" He did another back flip and smiled.

"Okay, I guess. Keffer it is! Now me." She again pointed to herself. "Lilly. Lilly."

"Lilly!" he shouted. "Lilly!" Another back flip and he was happy as a Lark. He hopped up onto a low-lying limb and shouted in a raspy voice, "Lilly! LILLY!" and pointed toward her.

What happened next took Lilly by utter surprise. At least a hundred other little voices shouted from the forest.

"Lilly! LILLY!"

Keffer wasn't the only Leafling near the Mirror Pool.

39

The Literati Elders had decided that the waiting game for answers to Tolk's riddles was frustrating. It was popular vote that this Shard, whatever type of jewel it must be, had to either be part of the meteor, or it was created during the burning crash of impact.

Elias had studied many old manuscripts, searching for an account of previous meteor crashes in known history. He only found mention of one other occurrence. It'd happened over one hundred years before, far north of Stone Castle in the wasteland known as The Dark Lands. It was stated that numerous jewels had been mined from that site of old, but nothing was mentioned about any of the jewels being Amethyst. No comments about any other sort of purple jewels were noted either. In fact, there was little to tell of that old crash site. It seems that most of the miners perished on site. The Dark Lands were full of dastardly creatures and evil unknown. Only a precious few workers returned from that trip. They brought with them several fine jewels, but they had paid a heavy price for them with the loss of so many lives. The writings stopped at that point in the story with no mention or description of the jewels found.

Probably the most perplexing question about the old writings was the fact that no other mention about leafy creatures were documented. No folklore ever emerged from that story other than its naming. It was called the Wrath of Fire. It was commonly assumed that the fire was the least of the damage done in that wretched wasteland. The deaths were most likely killings. No one dared to return, deeming that any other stones there would not be worth the search. News from that event only strengthened the fear of the townspeople in regard to the eeriness of that place. The northern lands were avoided at all costs.

Assuming that this meteor was a one-of-a-kind occurrence, they would approach its investigation with open minds. They vowed to document all they could about this meteor crash for future posterity and reference. But so far, there was little to scribe.

Despite the fact that Shark had no place in the hierarchy of Literati, his knowledge and common-sense approach to all things gave him worthy respect within the castle. He elected to take his men to return in four days. The moon would be fuller, offering more light if they needed to travel by night. Plus, his mind was as full as the others about this strange event. He didn't feel confident enough to make the trip again until he could reassure himself more so than now.

The Literati accepted his suggestions and waited impatiently for more answers.

Cobblestone Castle was making plans for return as well. Provisions had been secured, and the time was drawing near. The king's impatience was equally prominent as the Literati's. For reasons unknown to the king, his lower halls of the castle had flooded weekly since the meteor disaster. About when he was prepping for a trip to the site, another slight flood would put a few inches of water in the lower halls, requiring clean up. One of those times, it hadn't even rained—water seemed to come from out of nowhere. Then, for days, it'd be dry again. The castle had never experienced this before, and the king was pondering what had changed and how to stop it. Drainage around the castle seemed as perfect as before. It made no sense. It was as if something was trying to keep him too busy to set off on his exploration.

Perhaps someone was. Had he have known about the wonders of Aquavita, he might have understood his predicament and maybe even rethought his jewel endeavor. Alas, she can be quite crafty and sly when she wants to be. It's a good thing that he had not done anything to truly upset her as of yet. In such a case, subtlety was not a tool used by the Spirit of the Water.

So, days went by in both castles, as Lilly was at work and at play with her newly-found Leaflings. Her heart and mind pondered her part in this story. She felt small within a large tale, but for the time being, she had found a wonderland where she was truly happy. Her toughest question so far …

…what to do next?

40

Lilly spent her first day with the Leaflings learning what she could about them. There were so many, and each wanted their chance to spend some time with her. She had found them to be remarkably intelligent, mimicking some of Lilly's mannerisms and speech. Their minds were like sponges soaking up any tidbit of knowledge they could.

By day two, the Leaflings had learned many of her words and began using them even between themselves. They had learned *hello, please, thank you, come, rocks, water*, and a host of other simple words. She had helped her younger brother learn many words, but starting from scratch had proven difficult for her. A child can only learn at a certain rate, whereas these creatures advanced quickly, sometimes linking a few words into short sentences.

She, too, had learned. She listened closely to their noises and sounds. A hushing sound meant possible danger. Their coos seemed to reflect contentment, much like how a cat purrs when in a pleasant mood. Their arms and legs would motion one another directionally, which was learned primarily from watching Lilly. Learning communication was a labor of love between them all.

A particular question that Lilly couldn't seemed to convey to them was that of how they appeared here in this spot. For all the Leaflings knew, they had simply awakened and were part of the forest. When Lilly asked where their parents were, none had a reply. In fact, they had no idea what she even meant. "Parent?" Keffer would ask.

She had no way of describing the concept of child rearing. Apparently, none of them had been raised. This was evident in many ways. The really didn't know right from wrong other than the way it made them feel in their hearts. They would feel sadness and happiness, agitated, and sometimes even angered, but that was a trait still foreign to them. As of yet, they had not been crossed.

Their love of Lilly grew by the minute. They were fascinated by how and why she put nuts and berries in her mouth. She also had the same question of them and why they did not. She soon learned by watching that they would pause at certain times of the day and push their fingers and toes into the soil. They would assume a meditative state and sit quietly for minutes or hours at a time. At some point, they would pull their roots (or fingers and toes) from the ground and be on their merry way. It took Lilly a while to explain to them that she was essentially doing the same thing that they were, only in a different manner. There were comical confusions throughout the days. They were new friends learning another's way of life.

The Leaflings had another interesting habit that Lilly did not understand. At least once a day, they would, either individually or in groups, make their way to the waterfall for brief periods. Some would splash in behind the falls. Others would linger and mingle outside. For certain, at least daily, they would all do this. It was apparent that at some point, many more days would need to be spent with these wonderful creatures. There was just so much to learn about these special beings. They weren't human, and they certainly were plants, but they looked a little like both.

By the end of day two, Lilly felt as if she would need to share her finding of the Leaflings with someone else, most likely her family. She felt Aquavita had entrusted her to *something* with the Leaflings; she just didn't know what that was or how to go about it.

Perhaps a Leafling would travel home with her back to her home? Maybe Keffer. It might take some convincing to explain to the Leaflings about her intent. She didn't want them to feel like she had up and left them. She also didn't want the entire herd to tag along, which was very much a possibility. They were overly fond of her. They hadn't learned enough language to fully understand what was happening.

So, for the rest of the day and partially into the night, Lilly spoke to Keffer, helping him learn words and of her plan. She had gotten her point across to some degree and let Keffer share what he'd learned with the rest of his clan. They would leave early in the day and return as soon as possible. How much of that scenario Keffer actually understood was unknown, but Lilly felt confident that the two would leave a dawn. Since Lilly now knew the way, her travel should be quicker. They might even make it home just after dark. She fancied seeing the looks on the faces of her village when she strolled in with a living plant that talked! Her story was so unbelievable, that she'd have to have Keffer along with her just to prove truth to the matter.

She stretched out along the hillside near the Mirror Pool. It was so lovely with the stars reflecting off its surface. It was the prettiest place she'd ever been. Even her Iceland Pool home could not compare. She pulled her cloak over her body and shut her eyes. Her mind awash with ideas and possible plans, she was comforted knowing that tomorrow she would find help. The road would be long, but it would be worth it. What a journey it would be!

Unbeknownst to Lilly, the king would be traveling into the forest just as she was traveling out.

41

The following morning, Lilly and her new companion set off toward the Iceland Pool. She had carried Keffer for nearly an hour before realizing he could speed along even faster than she. His energy seemed endless as he bounced along the trail, swinging off limbs and bounding over rocks. Lilly raced along as fast as she could, stopping to rest periodically. The uphill was slow going. At least the second leg of her trail would be downhill.

By midday, the two had crested the mountain and looked out over the slopes of the mountain. Far in the distance, the Iceland Pool shimmered. A tiny waft of smoke could be seen from the campfires of home. It all looked so far away, but seeing signs of home renewed her vigor, plus the downhill sped up travel nicely.

They scampered along at a fair pace. Lilly had not noticed, but she had not been paying as close attention to her surroundings as she had on her other trips. She had begun to feel safe in the forest, and that can be quite dangerous. In her efforts to get home swiftly, she failed to realize she was being followed.

A silent set of eyes had been watching her every move.

* * *

As Lilly was making her way down the mountain, King Marcus' horses and men had reached the meteor site and what Lilly had called the Mirror Pool. They set up camp and unloaded their gear. Picks, shovels, hammers, and various other implements were piled just outside the cave entrance. Wooden kegs were full of oil, and large leather pouches contained dried sticks.

Protected from the water coming over the falls, these tools would be used to make torches. The men carted those inside the cave and began to investigate. Smaller hammers and chisels were the first tools to enter. As one team searched the cave tunnel, others had already begun tapping at the shiny stones along its walls and floors.

Inside two hours, they had already mined dozens of colorful stones. The king ran his fingers through the jewels, noting the quality and purity of what they'd found. He was quite pleased with this early outcome. This venture would definitely fund his city's rebuilding efforts, but more importantly, there would be plenty for he and his queen to share in the bounty!

"Keep digging, men! I'll send for wagons if I need to!"

* * *

Stone Castle was preparing for their next visit to the meteor site. In a couple of days, Shark and his boys would be leaving for that special waterfall. The Literati had poured over Tolk's writings with a fine-toothed comb. Elias and the Elders had made several notes for their travelers, hoping that any key words would help identify what they might find.

Their primary list included a few precise words of Tolk. Myrtos (Myrtle), walking feet and hands, Mirare', Shard of Amethyst, She (in whom they should trust), and a series of rhyming quatrains. It all looked like gibberish on parchment, but it was what they had to go on. Two more days, and they would depart.

The head chef at the Stone Castle had begun baking special foods that could last for longer than a few days. No one knew how long the team would be gone, so food was of paramount interest … especially for Claybon. He'd already been stashing back dried meats and wax-coated cheeses in his own private pouches. The boy didn't miss many meals.

The Elders were more than ready for the three to embark, but Shark was steadfast that he would know when the time was right.

Eventually, he would.

42

The sun had already set, and darkness had fallen as Lilly and Keffer saw the light of the campfire shining through the trees. They had made it home in record time. Lilly was exhausted but exhilarated by being home. Even the Leafling had finally started to show signs of tiring. The light from the fire startled him and he jumped into Lilly's arms.

"What's the matter, Keffer? Its alright! This is home for me!"

Keffer wasn't so sure and continued to cling to her neck, nestled under the safety of her hair. His little head peered out between the strands of hair and flowers.

"Momma! Poppa! Kato!"

A roar of enthusiasm came out of the village as Lilly's family rushed out to meet her. She paused, panting from her run, then hugged each one with happiness and love. Not one of them took note of stick of myrtle wound into her hair.

"We are so glad you are home! You are back quicker than we expected!" her father said.

"Poppa, Momma, I found what I was supposed to find!"

All grew excited with eyes wide open.

"I found them ... but I don't know what I'm supposed to do next. I ... I need help."

All waited on pins and needles while Lilly found the proper words.

"I ... I found ... well, I guess I should just show you." She walked over near the light of the campfire and motioned the others near. She lifted a tuft of her hair, held out her hand, and spoke. "Come on, Keffer. Its okay. You're safe."

Somehow, a stick fell out of her hair and onto her palm. "Its okay, Keffer. Tell them hello."

On its own accord, the stick raised and stood up onto its feet. To her family's astonishment, the stick spoke!

"Hello! I'm Keffer."

Lilly's parents took a step back in awe.

Kato began to jump up and down. "Can I hold it! Can I hold it! Pleeeease!"

Lilly and Keffer both smiled and the young one's antics. Lilly lowered her hand and extended it to Kato. Unexpectedly, Keffer jumped onto Kato's arm and scampered up into his hair and mimicked the hugs he'd witnessed a moment ago. Kato placed his palm against the Leafling, trying to offer a return hug.

"Lilly, can we keep him!"

Lilly chuckled out loud. "He's our friend, Kato! He's not a pet, but if it makes you feel better, he seems quite fond of you!"

Keffer burrowed his head into Kato's neck once more and smiled. He then bounced over to Lilly's father and attempted the same hug. This startled her father, and he pushed Keffer back down his arm. "How do we know this thing is safe?"

"Oh, Poppa," she chirped. "I've been with them for two days and with him today also. I'm helping them learn to talk."

Although Keffer hadn't learned all that many words yet, he did understand many. He looked up at her father and tilted his head. "Keffer good! Love!"

Lilly's mother spoke up. "Don't look at me! I don't need to pet anything! What in the world have you gotten us into, child?"

"Momma, I don't know what to do. He's not the only one! There's a whole bunch! The woods is full! All sizes ... big, small, you name it!"

The barrage of questions continued for another hour until they all sat down by the fire to put a plan together. Lilly's father was ready to do anything for his girl, but her mother was a different story.

"This is what comes of tarrying off into the unknown!" she grumbled.

"Momma, look at the wonderful creature. How can you not want to help him and his kind? You raised me to be compassionate. I'm overflowing with it right now. Just please give me some ideas."

It was her father's turn to talk. "You're right, Lilly. We must do something. Hummm." He scratched his chin as he thought. "I think this is more than we know how to handle. Well, it seems you've made friends with those Literati folk. That seems logical to me. Ask the wise men."

Lilly couldn't believe she had not thought of that. Of course, he was right! "Yes, Poppa! The Literati are wise. They'll know what to do! I'll go in the morning! Thank you, Poppa!"

"Hold on, little lady. Perhaps the first part of your quest was meant to be alone. I think it's high time I went along."

"Oh, would you, Poppa?"

He gave her a nod and a smile. "I will go."

"I'm going!" shouted Kato.

"Kato is not going," grumbled his mother.

Lilly's father raised an eyebrow. "Now Nelly, your children are both supposed to play a part in this story. Aquavita requested them both, if you recall. How can I forbid him going?"

Nelly huffed and shook her head. "Oh, you Riverpools! Oh! Why, my own mother would turn in her grave! You'll get us all killed! Why, I never!"

Lilly and her parents were so wrapped up in their conversations, that they didn't realize Keffer and Kato had slipped off to the water's edge. A quick scan of the riverbank located the two. As Lilly and her parents eased toward them, they soon noticed that something was going on there. Both were crouched at the water's edge, their faces near its surface. Kato was whispering beneath his breath with his eyes closed. Keffer was cooing ever so quietly. Both stopped simultaneously and peered back over their shoulders at the others. Kato spoke up.

"We leave in the morning. The water says we go."

The leafling smiled at Kato, then looked back at them and spoke.

"Yes! What ***he*** said."

* * *

The lone individual that had followed Lilly all day was now nestled into the woods nearby, still watching and still listening to every word. With a wry smile, he thought to himself …

"… looks like another long walk tomorrow."

43

The king had worked his men all through the night. In his mindset, it was already dark inside the cave, so there was no need for daylight. He'd already sent news back to Cobblestone Castle to send more men for rotations digging in the cave. Each new pouch of jewels pulled from the tunnel sent his emotions to a higher level. Rubies, Sapphires, Emeralds, Diamonds. This was the greatest treasure hoard any king had pilfered in Cobblestone's documented history. The deeper the workers delved, the larger the jewels were. It was as if the slowing of the meteor had let it linger longer as it pressed through the soil, melting with both heat and pressure. Excitement was building.

Just a sun's morning light was beginning to shine through the trees, two workers left the cave and approached the king.

"Sire, the end of the tunnel is different than the rest of the cave passage. It terminates in a cavern large enough to stand in. There is a ball of black rock at the bottom that weighs too much to carry. Nothing about it sparkles. It's just a shiny black ore probably three feet across."

"Then roll it out. Inch it upward, blocking it as you need rest. Rotate men. Roll some more. Bring it into the light."

The men nodded, dreading the uphill battle between men and stone. Alas, they knew that the king's words were not a request. They would either roll it out or die trying.

The two reentered the cave, pausing to cool themselves and rinse off the dirt and ash in the waterfall entrance.

Hours passed. By midafternoon, the enormously heavy stone rolled through the waterfall and out into sunlight. Farther along the shoreline, the workers brought it to rest and shored up the base. Then, with hammer and chisel, sledgehammer and ax, they began chipping away at the black ore. It was unbelievably hard. Every tiny chip from its surface was hard-earned. As one man would tire, another would stand in and take over. One of the men was badly injured when his chisel slid from the stone. His hammer smashed into his hand, shattering several bones, and cutting his skin badly. They bound his hand, placed him on horseback and sent him back to Cobblestone for medical attention. No one could take time from the project to ensure he would make it back without passing out, or worse yet, dying. Nothing was too paramount to override this project.

Still, they chipped away. Still, more jewels came up through the tunnel. Still, the king smiled, utterly thrilled with his finds.

44

Daybreak found the Riverpool family packed and walking toward Stone Castle. Lilly led the caravan, being the only one familiar with the trail. It was only a few days prior that Shark and Daniel had led Lilly from Stone Castle into the valley of the Iceland Pool. This day would find them backtracking over those same footsteps.

Kato and Keffer followed Lilly. The two of them jabbered continuously as they walked. Kato was elated with his new friend, and Keffer was piecing together sentences as he learned more words. Kato kept reminding Lilly, "This is a grand adventure, Lilly! Grand!"

Her father took up the rear, every now and then casting a sheepish glance over at his wife, Nelly. She'd wrinkle her nose, muttering to herself. "Humph. Tarrying off with the likes of Tucker Riverpool. If this isn't a goose chase, I've never seen one. Why, I never …"

There were times when Nelly sure sounded gruff, but old Tucker had learned to let her chides slide off like water from a duck's back. The two had clearly paired for life, it just didn't always sound like it.

Lilly had hoped to make a faster trek along the trail, but the additional travelers had slowed the pace. She'd also noticed that Keffer was looking more tired than when they'd first met. Perhaps yesterday's long travel was a bit much for him. After all, he couldn't be very old. He must have been born, hatched, or reared in some way last week. The more she thought, the more questions she had.

By late afternoon, they'd crested the mountain and bared right upon the Old Road. The walking would be much flatter than the uphill climb they'd just ascended. Lilly took a short break to let them all rest.

The Leafling never really appeared winded from their climb, but he was clearly tired from the trek. He was still in great spirits and enjoying time with Kato, but the trip was wearing on him.

Another few hours of travel led them past where the injured old troll had been lying. She had told the story to her parents a few days ago, and now she mentioned it again, showing them where he'd been. "Ravok was his name. Perhaps Shark and Daniel were able to drag him to Stone Castle. Someone must have helped him. He's not here anymore." As the crew walked past where the troll had suffered, Lilly couldn't help feeling a pang of sorrow for him. The blackish-red bloodstained grass was a bitter enough reminder, but the stories he told about his shattered life rang in her head. She finally turned her attention to the road ahead. It was a calm day and not overly hot. It made the long day more bearable.

"We should be to Stone Castle in a couple of hours." The family nodded in agreement, looking forward to trail's end. By now, Lilly had gotten used to long days on her feet, but her family rarely paced farther than the half-mile stretch along their shoreline. Kato didn't seem to mind. His new best friend and he hadn't stopped chatting since they'd left the Iceland Pool.

Lilly spoke some more. "I'm sure we will be quite a sight for the Literati, but I'm certain they will welcome us. They've been desperate for information about the meteor and all the things that have happened since the crash. I think meeting Keffer will piece together many parts of their puzzle."

Tucker spoke up. "What do you think they will tell us? I don't even know what to ask them."

"I don't think we will have to ask them much, Poppa. These men are very, very wise. They're our only hope."

"I can't lie, sweetheart," he replied. "I'm a little nervous about meeting them. Our custom is to fear them. And there's another thing. Maybe I'm just paranoid, but I feel like we are being watched. Do they have watchers in the woods here?"

"Don't worry, Poppa," she commented, "Look at the bright side. The baker at Stone Castle will serve us some of the best food you'll ever put in your mouth. I can't wait for you to try their bread. It's wonderful!"

"What's your little friend eat?" he asked.

Lilly had been so caught up in thought to think about Keffer's food needs. They stopped at a small puddle along the road, and Lilly pointed it out to the Leafling. He quickly scampered over to the water and slid his fingers and toes into its mud. "Ah," the creature commented, as if he were a human slipping into a bath. Surely, this was why Keffer had looked so tired. He had not absorbed any nutrients for a couple days. *This should perk him up*, she thought.

Although anxious to be on their way, they let the Leafling take in a good soaking. Soon, he doused his head with water and shook off his limbs. With a quirky smile, he jumped up onto Kato and stated, "Go now! Happy."

They continued their trek. Lilly's father kept looking off into the forest, half expecting to see someone or something watching their moves. He could sense eyes upon them. He kept his bamboo handy and hoped he wouldn't have to use it. It was an eerie feeling, but he kept a watchful eye and walked along attentively.

Tucker Riverpool was right.

Something was watching them.

45

Lilly and family neared Stone Castle before sunset. Tucker and Nelly were exhausted. And strangely, little Keffer was uncharacteristically quiet. He, too, was tired from the travel. Lilly had thought that the time in the mud puddle would have strengthened him, but it had made little difference. Thankfully, the castle was now in view. The Literati could surely help.

"Lilly!" came a shout in the distance. "It's you!"

Master Daniel had been manning the watch out front of the castle. Despite the camouflage of their attire, he spotted her and came running to great her. He could see that she had company, but all he really saw was her. She had been weighing heavily on his mind since they'd left her in her village by the lake. He had loved their time together, and he thought of it often. Without another greeting, he raced up to her and gave her a big hug.

"It's wonderful to see you!" he said, smiling ear to ear.

Lilly wasn't quite prepared for such a hug, but it felt grand to her. Despite the whirlwind of her recent days, she, too, had thought about their time together as well. She blushed a little as her family watched the greeting. Lilly gave a quick glance toward her mother. Nelly raised an eyebrow and gave a knowing smile. Lilly turned her glance away and back to Daniel.

"It's good to see you, too, Daniel."

"What ever are you doing so far from home? I mean … how can I help you? I'm sure you're tired and hungry."

"We are definitely both, but we very much need to see the Literati. We have a … well … we need help."

"Of course, come along."

Lilly's group followed Daniel to the castle. They exchanged introductions along the way. Daniel was pleased to oblige them all. Even entering the castle, he still hadn't noticed the leafy stick riding upon Kato's shoulder. It was quite a sight, a full pod of Wild Folk stepping into the castle. Most inside gave a double take and stared at these new quests. Daniel spoke to his brethren.

"We have guests, men. They wish to speak to us. They are in need of help. Could someone gather the Elders?"

Daniel led the group to the council hall, giving them a seat. He motioned to the castle chef to bring food and drink as Literati and students gathered to see what Lilly and crew had to say. Though Lilly's last visit was short, she'd made quite an impression on them all, with Daniel being her biggest fan.

As Daniel and Lilly caught up on the last few days, food was brought and sat before them. The Elders arrived and called an official council to hear what Lilly had to say.

"Miss Riverpool. What can we of the Literati do for you?" asked Elias.

Lilly began. "I have a thousand things to tell you, but I'll start with the most pressing. I've been to the meteor site and spent a couple of days there. It was there that I discovered something you need to be aware of, and more importantly, we need help deciding what to do about it."

The Literati sat silent, letting her find her words. For the lack of proper description, she simply stated. "I found these." She looked over to Keffer and spoke to him.

"Keffer, could you come and say hello to everyone?"

To the astonishment of the entire crowd, part of Kato's cloak disguise hopped off his shoulder and onto the table. With a glance around the room, Keffer spoke.

"Hello, I'm Keffer. Love." He gave a slight bow as he scanned the room once more.

Gasps filled the room. Eyes widened.

"My word!" exclaimed Elias. "What is this?!"

As the crowd quieted, all still stared in disbelief, creeping closer for a better look. Keffer took a few steps side to side, looking back and Lilly time and again. Ordinarily, he would have done a quick back flip (per his custom), but the Leafling felt lackluster and lethargic. He'd never felt this way before. Usually his energy was overflowing, but not this day. Lilly spoke up again.

"He is not the only one. There are many near the Mirror Pool and around the waterfall. I have found them harmless, but I don't know much about them other than what you see here. They've been ever so friendly to me … and so very curious. They've learned many words of our language in just a few days. They are very intelligent."

Lilly let those words soak into the crowd for a moment and then continued.

"They have sounds of their own to communicate. It sounds like … well … like a …"

She struggled for a proper word to adequately describe the Leaflings native tongue.

"Like a coo," inserted Claybon. "I heard them when we were there, I just didn't see them."

"Yes," Lilly replied. "A coo. And I have another issue. Keffer, this one, has become weak on this trip. He usually has plenty of energy, but his condition has gotten worse as we've traveled. I'm worried about him, and the others, too. It's why I came here. We hope you have knowledge of what we must do."

Elias had been quiet, letting Lilly give her speech. Several others had started asking questions of her and among themselves. Elias had paced over to the open window and was staring out into the forest in deep thought. When he finally broke his silence, he began reciting Tolk's writings and adding his own thoughts.

"Through fiery night it fell, as if from burning Hell. It scorched into the ground to places still unfound. They raised their roots from land and walked on foot and hand. And raised by human fist, came the Shard of Amethyst. Myrtos, Mirare." He then spoke his own thoughts aloud.

"Scorched into the ground. Heat and pressure make jewels. A shard of Amethyst would be the very core of the meteor. It would have energy radiating from it, enhancing the forest in many ways. It has awakened the trees! The myrtos! *Nurture the Myrtos* ... I now understand. Nurture means more than planting and watering trees and vines. Nurture, in this case, means raise them like a child. Teach them. Can you imagine what we could learn from them! This is it! This is what Tolk meant."

He looked to Lilly with a warm smile. "Trust in SHE, for without her, they shall not be. Welcome, Lilly Riverpool. We trust you."

Lilly was bewildered with Elias' assessment. It had filled in many blanks for her, but it was a lot to take in.

"You mentioned the Mirror Pool, as you've named it. Tolk deemed it Mirare', meaning mirror. Your descriptions are perfect, Lilly. He named the place Tal Kator, which I did not understand at first. Tal is short for the Greek term, telesma, a religious rite of awakening. Kator is another Greek term short for Catastrephine, or catastrophe. Together, they simply mean new life from disaster. It makes perfect sense."

"But why is my friend sick?" asked Lilly.

"The answer is simple, Lilly. He gets his strength from the Shard. He must rejuvenate himself near it soon, or he will parish."

Lilly jumped from her chair. "Perish?! Then I'll take him now!"

"There will not be need of that tonight in the dark. At first light, we will help you get him there." Elias turned his attention to his crowd.

"Prepare, men. Gather supplies. I will be making this journey along with our original group of three, as well as this family. Others may come, but most must stay behind to care for the castle and keep it safe from intrusion. Understood?"

Many of the men raced off to make preparations. The Elders remained and continued to converse with Lilly and her family. Elias still had numerous other quotes of Tolk on his mind, which he intended to ask yet this evening. One particular quote was forefront.

"Lilly, Tolk told us to split the Shard. Until this moment, I had no idea why we would do such a thing, even if we actually found it. But now I understand. By splitting the Shard, part of it would remain here and the other part would be left there in Tal Kator. If the Literati are to nurture them—teach them the ways of the world, the creatures would need to be able to come here for learning. We would also need to go there. By splitting the Shard, they will flourish in which ever location they are. Two worlds for them in which to grow and learn."

"Lilly," he continued.

"This is going to be glorious!"

46

As the first hint of morning light pierced the panes of Stone Castle, Lilly's group and six Literati left the castle toward the meteor site, which they were now calling Tal Kator. Their pace was as quick as possible, wanting to get Keffer back home to his fellow Leaflings. Kato was carrying him now. His condition had weakened almost to the point of wilting. As they walked, Lilly would pet his leaves and reassure him that he would feel better soon.

Elias came along on this venture just as he had suggested. It was difficult for him to keep up with the rest of the crew. He was in his late seventies, and his old bones did not scurry along as quickly as the rest.

Shark led the way, being overly cautious as usual. All were anxious to reach their destination.

* * *

The early morning sun reflected from the surface of the Mirare'. The king's men were still packing out bags of jewels from the cavern behind the waterfall. Another group was pounding away at the large, black stone just outside of the cave. They'd made some progress and had managed to chip a divot into the top of the stone, preparing for a large chisel wedge and a much larger hammer. Soon, the hole in its surface was large enough to settle in the chisel. It stood upright on its own, where no hands could be injured by the hammer about to strike blows.

One of the king's largest men raised high his sledge. With all the force he could muster, he thrust down onto the chisel. His hammer bounced from its surface and nearly left his grip. He summoned up for another strike. Again, the hammer bounced from the chisel backward toward its user. He pulled together every ounce of energy he had from within and made a roundhouse swing. The hammer landed squarely upon the chisel with utter force.

CRACK!

The sound of the stone breaking in two was piercing to the ears of all who witnessed it. Each half of the meteor's core toppled open like a coconut. Its hollow interior glistened with tiny crystal-clear stones. It resembled a giant geode split in two. Nestled within one of the stone halves like a peach seed rested a large purple stone. The sunlight pierced its colorful surface, giving off rays of glorious purple light. Its surface sparkled.

The King had seen Amethyst stones before, but never one of such size and magnitude. Everyone stared in wide wonder.

"Wow!" exclaimed the king, "Now that's a jewel!" He walked over to the core of the meteor and gazed at his prize. How wonderous! He reached into the broken stone shell and plucked out the stone. It was warm to the touch, and it filled his entire hand. He immediately felt a surge of energy pulsing through his body. It was exhilarating and rejuvenating at the same time. Even the men nearby could feel a tingling within their bodies.

It was hours before the king would release his grip on the shard. He sat silently upon a nearby rock ledge and stared into its nearly transparent surfaces. He had instructed his people to carry on with their mining. All the while, he could not pull his eyes from it.

"Glorious!" he whispered to himself.

"Absolutely Glorious!"

* * *

Early afternoon found Lilly's crew nearing Tal Kator. Shark and his two students remembered the path from only a few days before.

The closer they came to the Mirare', the more Keffer's condition improved. He could feel his strength returning, and it showed. Lilly and Kato were relieved. The Literati smiled with appreciation as well, reassured that their assessment of the effect of the Shard upon the Leaflings was correct.

As they neared the Mirare', an unsettling noise was heard. There were voices and the sounds of clinking hammers and chisels. In an instant, Elias knew what was occurring.

"It's the king and his men," Elias grumbled with a scowl. "They are mining jewels."

They crested a ridge and peered down into the crater hole that was now the sparkling lake of the Mirare'. Around its banks were several men carrying tools and heavy pouches. It was quite obvious what the king was doing.

The group descended the hillside trail and walked up to the king and his men. Distracted with work, none saw them coming. The king, still mesmerized by his gem, only looked up when he heard Elias' voice.

"Your Highness! I wish I'd known you were excavating. I should have liked to have seen your finds."

"Well, Elias!" replied the king, "I hardly expected to see you wandering out this far from the castle! I have been quite busy with the restoration of our city and failed to inform you of our plan to mine this site."

Elias listened intently, fully knowing that the king was not telling the whole truth. "I have no doubt, Your Highness, that the restoration of Cobblestone has kept you quite busy, but I suspect you wanted to keep this little venture quite secret."

The King gave a crafty smile. "Yes, yes, you've got me there, Elias. A venture of this magnitude requires a certain amount of secrecy, as you might expect. Do tell, Elias … what is the purpose of your expedition on this day."

Elias paused, waiting for the proper words. "We are on a mission for a number of things, Sire. As you are well aware, we of the Literati are always in search of knowledge … answers to the unknowns. In this case, there are many unknowns."

The king listened intently, sizing up Elias and his crew. "Go on, Elias. I'm all ears."

"You see, Your Highness, this meteor has impacted this forest in many ways. With all due respect, Sire, you have overlooked some important details in your haste to mine jewels."

"I don't care for your tone, Elias. You are addressing your king, and I suggest you choose your words carefully."

"Then I will cut to the chase, Your Majesty. This meteor awakened the forest in such a way as never before. Have you not noticed how quickly the woods has begun to regrow? Plants are springing from piles of ash! The meteor has changed the landscape here not only in the terrain, but in its chemical makeup as well. The forest has changed!"

"Oh, Elias, I have little interest in the pathways of water or the resprouting of trees. I am here to gather jewels to help aid my endeavors to rebuild Cobblestone."

Elias gave a reply. "It seems you have many pouches of jewels already that should fetch quite the fortune. That is good for us all, honestly. We all want a well-fortified rulership for protection and care of our fair city. We are not here to interrupt your quest in that regard. We have an equally important dilemma. I don't have all the answers yet, but I have reason to believe that the heart of this meteor is what has changed these surroundings. The core of the meteor gives off energy … energy that is like nothing we've ever known."

"I continue to listen, Elias, but my patience grows thin. As you can see, I have mining to do."

Elias looked to the ground near the king. Both haves of the meteor core still lay where the king's men had cracked it open. "It appears, King Marcus, that you have already found the object of which we seek. Tell me, Your Highness, did the stone within this stone shell at your feet glow gloriously purple?"

The king was impressed with Elias' knowledge about this site. How could Elias have known what was inside that meteor core? He simply had to ask. "How is it that you know so much about this meteor, Elias? You told me, via the Tower Ravens, that you knew very little about it. Now, it seems, you are quite the scholar upon the subject."

"We are only now deciphering Tolk's final scribing. His work was vague and difficult to understand. All of his odd clues came to clarity with the arrival of this young lady beside me. She and her family came to the castle last night with news and proof of what Tolk was trying to say. It made sense to me in an instant. I would have sent word to you instantly after this quest. You have my word on that, Your Highness."

The king's temper was rising. "So you've come to pilfer the king's soil, have you? That would be theft and perhaps treason! Shall I hang you here, or drag you to Cobblestone for all to see?"

Shark could no longer hold back the anger brewing inside. "We have stolen nothing!" he shouted.

The king gave Shark a scowl. "It seems you know me, but I have not been granted the respect of making your acquaintance!"

"Your men know me, King Marcus, even if you do not!"

One of the king's men spoke up. "Your Highness, his name is Shark. He is a sailor out of the Bay of Greenwale. More likely a pirate, I'd say, I would."

"Well, Shark, you may hang as well!"

Shark was already reaching for the hilt of his sword when Elias stayed his hand.

Elias addressed the king again. "Your Highness, please! We did not come here to steal. We came to find the source of what has awakened the forest."

Unbeknownst to Elias and his crew, the king had quickly wrapped the Shard in a cloth when Elias' intrusion happened. He had kept it behind his back while talking. During the conversation with Elias, he had jostled it into view of his men. Quietly, one had slipped up behind him and slipped the stone from his grasp and backed away from the crowd. During the commotion, no one noticed the man easing the Shard into one of the horse's saddle bags. Slowly, he eased away from the crowd, leading the horse to the path to Cobblestone, while King Marcus held everyone's attention.

This *awakening* nonsense had the king furious. "What has awakened!?!" he shouted. "I see nothing here but trees and birds! This is preposterous!"

Lilly had been too overwhelmed to say a word before now. She tugged on Kato's arm, and they both stepped out in front of Elias and Shark. She gently bowed toward the king and said, "Your Highness, I am Lilly from the Iceland Pool. I offer this to you as proof of the awakening."

She extended her hand toward the king and nodded to Kato. She said, "Come on, Keffer. It's okay."

The Leafling bounced from Kato's shoulder and onto Lilly's arm. He mimicked the bowing gesture Lilly had given and spoke to the king. "I'm Keffer! Love!"

The king and all of his men were astounded. There was complete silence for a moment while the king grasped for words. With a distasteful frown, the king finally spoke up.

"What new devilry have you conjured, Elias? What spells have you Warlocks cast upon the forest!?!"

"Your Highness!" exclaimed Elias. "This is not devilry! This is new life created by the very stone you have unearthed here in the forest. It is their life source."

The king still struggled for words as he crept closer to the Leafling, eyeing it tip to toe. "So, this Shard you tell me of … its energy is what feeds this stick creature?"

Elias replied, "Yes, Sire. To my limited knowledge, the heart of the meteor is its livelihood."

The wheels were turning in the king's mind. "So…" he continued, "if it offers such wondrous effects for this tiny thing, imagine what the stone could do for me?"

The king's comment was a complete surprise to Elias and company. They had hoped to sway the king, not rally his greed!

The king began to speak quietly, almost to himself, yet aiming his words more or less toward Elias. "The stone … it was warm to the touch … I felt that energy emitting from it. It is priceless!"

Elias tried to break the spell the stone had over the king. "Your Highness, you have countless jewels from this mine that are worth untold fortunes! You mustn't keep it for yourself! It belongs here in the forest …right here where it landed! The forest needs it!"

"Quiet!" the King shouted. "I would not forfeit such a priceless jewel to save one tiny talking stick! Imagine the power that will be mine! For NO purpose would I relinquish the Shard!"

Lilly interrupted the king's rant. "It's not one little stick, Your Highness."

Lilly peered down into Keffer's eyes and spoke to him. "Lilly … Lilly …" she whispered.

Keffer smiled and nodded. He then shouted his raspy call. "LILLY! LILLY!"

One second later, a wave of rustling sound rushed across the forest floor and throughout the trees. With a roar, the forest shouted back to Keffer.

"LILLY! LILLY!"

Within seconds, the same rushing wave of noise swarmed the confines of the Mirare'. In all directions, high and low, Leaflings clung to everything. Hundreds, perhaps thousands of leafy creatures of different sizes and shapes all came into view. As quickly as they came, the Leaflings fell utterly silent as if waiting further instructions.

The king had maintained his composure. Whether he was calculating a plan, or perhaps still reeling from his dreamy fantasies about the Shard, he meticulously spoke again to the crowd.

"I must admit, Lilly from the Iceland Pool, you put on quite a show. Tell me, little one, what do I, King of Cobblestone, have to fear from a rustling pile of leaves?"

"Your Highness," she replied, "I do not know what they are capable of. In fact, I doubt they know either. They are young, having had no upbringing. They just appeared. Who knows what will happen if they are angered!"

The king still wore his smug and candied smile. "You see, there is a tiny piece of information you simply do not have! Even if I wanted to relinquish my newly acquired stone … which I do not, by the way … it is not currently in my possession! It has long since been on its way to Cobblestone … to a secure location that only I know! Brilliant tactic, wouldn't you agree?"

The king could only admire his own brilliance in this situation. He chuckled as he spoke. "Ha! So, what are you going to do? Throw leaves at me until I give up the secret location? Harming me would only ensure that you never find out its location! Ha!"

At that very moment, a scream and a thud were heard down the trail toward Cobblestone. As the crowd around the Mirare' gazed back toward the sound, hoof steps could be heard coming closer to them. To everyone's surprise, it was the king's horse with its rider bound and tied to the horse's back. It was being led by a very large troll. The troll walked with a bit of a limp as it led horse and rider back to the Mirare'.

It was Ravok! It had been he who had been following Lilly and family for days. Out of respect and honor toward Lilly's medical help, he had taken on the charge of looking after Lilly as a means of repaying her for her kindness. A full smile graced his face for the first time in decades, and it was a true smile of happiness. It was perhaps the happiest he had ever been. Lilly's simple act of kindness had changed the troll's whole point of view on life. Much of the bitterness had left his heart, and he was elated to return Lilly's favor. He hobbled past the King, horse, saddle bags, and all. Even injured, Ravok still looked formidable and enormous to this crowd. He stopped in front of Lilly and spoke.

"One good deed deserves another, Lilly Riverpool. I believe this belongs to you, my lady." He handed her the reins as everyone there pondered their next moves in silence.

Lilly gave the troll a heartfelt smile as a tear slid down her cheek. "You're alive, Ravok! I don't know how to thank you!"

"It is I who owe the thanks, Miss Lilly. You've shown me many things."

The king, still furious, addressed Lilly.

"I have to hand it to you, Lilly from the Iceland Pool, you are a woman of many surprises. But, surely you realize that one crippled troll and a pile of leaves would not be much of a match for me and my men."

Before Lilly could answer, Shark stepped forward.

"She has my sword!"

Lilly's father stepped forward.

"She has our bamboo!"

As the stalemate continued, the king gritted his teeth in fury.

"Fear not, Little Lady. No need to muster your band of ramshackle ruffians. This day obviously belongs to you! No need to take up arms this day. It would only add to your list charges! In fact, take my horse as well! It'll give my old friend, Elias, a comfortable ride back to Stone Castle."

The king paused to let his angry words soak in. He continued.

"But, rest assured, Lilly Riverpool, I WILL return … and when I do … I will bring with me an army liken to nothing you've ever seen before. Enjoy this minimal victory, for my revenge will be relentless."

The king meant what he said. He would take back the Shard by force, by detestable means. Unless something miraculous took place to change the king's heart, his words would come true with a vengeance.

But miracles sometimes happen …

With the king's last words, yet another surprising occurrence unfolded. A dark cloud appeared above the Mirare', and with it, a rumble was felt in the earth beneath the surface of the Mirare'. Ripples swelled across the surface of the lake, and a cool and humid wind drifted through the forest. The rumbles grew louder. Ripples became waves along the shore.

The wind began to swirl in the center of the Mirare', and water began to rise from its surface.

Only Lilly and Kato could foresee what would happen next.

Elias' voice quivered, "What's happening!?!"

Lilly looked up to Elias with a crafty smile.

"I forgot to tell you about Aquavita …"

47

The spire of water rising from the Mirare' was nothing short of miraculous. As the being known as Aquavita began to take form, all stood in wonder at the glorious site. The funnel of angered water rose far higher than when she had shown herself to Lilly and Kato several days before. Upward the water pushed until the form of Aquavita was evident to all. The angered emotion she wore on her face reflected nothing like Lilly's memory of her. She had taken the form of wrath today, and it was frightening to behold.

And behold, she spoke.

"King Marcus of Cobblestone!" she shouted.

Even the mighty stature of King Marcus cowered beneath the splendor of Aquavita. He could not speak, shaking as her words pierced his soul.

"YOU! King Marcus! Your greed has clouded your judgement! Where is the common sense and valor you once emitted! Where is your HONOR?!!"

Her voice pounded through the chests of all witnessing her wrath. Her voice, though feminine, had an impact like thunder. Her commonly pure and gentle voice had swollen to tidal proportions. Even Lilly and Kato feared what she was capable of doing.

"SPEAK!" she shouted to the King.

The king could not utter a word. He tried, but fear had embraced him fully.

Aquavita's voice quieted as she bent down to his level, eyeing him closely. "Very well, then. I will speak for you, and YOU will understand your place in this story. You WILL do as I speak, or I will smite you down like a fly beneath my fist!"

As she shouted, her arm drew high and a snarl like thunder escaped her lips. "Hear me, King Marcus!"

The king, still shaking head to toe, did his best to look her in the eye as she spoke.

Aquavita settled into a smaller shape, her waters easing back into the pool from whence she came. She now stood slightly taller than the king, and her words softened.

"Your greed has clouded your judgement. You are the valiant King with honor. You are strong of will to protect your city. You have humility to address your civilians. In your heart, you still have compassion. You still have all of the qualities of a fair and just king. You must use those qualities like you once did."

The king still stood bewildered, his legs trembling beneath him. In his heart, he knew she was right. It took the sheer force of Aquavita to get him to realize what he had become. The spoils of being King had only fueled his inner fire for more. His position had changed him inside. It took the magnitude of a situation like this to shake him back to his old self. Fear can be a great motivator, and it had motivated the king.

Aquavita sensed that she had struck a chord in the king. Her own compassion allowed her to settle her anger and return to her common state. Her currents flowed up around the king, embracing him like a child. Her words were now soft and motherly.

"Go now, Fair King! Take these jewels and repair your city. Govern like you once did. Let valor and honor be your guide. Lead by example."

The king finally uttered three words. "Who are you?"

Aquavita chuckled. "Your new friends over there will tell you all about me. And remember … listen to the water when you are troubled. I will be there … just as I always have been."

With those words, Aquavita swirled away from the king. She gazed over to Lilly and family. Warm hues of color flushed her face as she spoke.

"Well done, Friends! I am so very proud of all of you! Work together … all of you. You will not need me, but I will be nearby. Listen for me, for I will be listing for you."

Kato spoke up, tears overflowing.

"Don't go, Aquavita! Don't go!"

Aquavita smiled and touched his face with her watery hand.

"Young Kato! You will always be in my heart. You will hear me when you wish, just as you always have."

She turned to Lilly. "You've done well, my special one. You are mighty for one so small." Her smile beamed in glorious shades.

"Thank you, Aquavita," Lilly spoke through the tears. "I will miss you."

"Oh, my Lilly, I will never be far from you!"

As her currents began to swirl away, she glanced toward Elias.

"Nurture the Myrtos, Elias!"

Elias was overwhelmed. Just the fact that she had called to him melted his heart. This was a story like he could never have imagined.

The king and his men still stared in wonder, not knowing for certain what they should do next. The king spoke up with a smile.

"Ugh, Ma'am … so I can keep the other jewels?"

Aquavita chuckled out loud.

"Yes, Marcus, you can keep the jewels. Just not the pretty purple one!"

With that, Aquavita swirled herself back into the Miraré. The ripples on the water diminished, and the clouds dissipated. The wind drifted away, and the forest grew calm again.

Lilly's crew all hugged, tears of happiness flowing freely among them.

Lilly was so filled with excitement and joy that without even giving it a thought, she turned to Daniel and kissed him in celebration. Daniel blushed several shades of red as he stood in amazement. His broad smiled opened up as she released her kiss. Although a bit awkward, it was still quite magical. He finally uttered a few words.

"Just when I thought the day couldn't possibly get any more amazing …"

48

To say that the conditions after the disappearance of Aquavita were an awkward situation would be an extreme understatement. Numerous walks of life that were arch enemies only minutes prior, were now trying to come to terms with how to move forward in a positive way. Each were inspired to utilize this supernatural occurrence for the betterment of the common good as well as the betterment of their own souls, but eyeing an age-old arch enemy with good favor is tough, at best. It would take time to fully digest all of what happened on this special day, but for the moment, the strangeness of everything that had happened was all encompassing.

Ravok was not the least of these. Here was an individual that had spent his entire life in envy and distrust of others. Bitterness had followed his every move since childhood. In his life, there had only been ugliness and despair. Disappointment and sorrow followed his every move. Lack of love, lack of friendship, lack of companionship … it all spelled discomfort for him. A pleasant atmosphere never graced his daily routine. Joy was ever elusive. Now, he was faced with the opportunity to change all that, but how? He desperately wanted to talk to Lilly, but everyone else did too at this point.

That is … if anyone could pry her from the embrace of Daniel. The two sparkled in that special moment for a few seconds before the onslaught began.

Of course, the king took precedence overall. When one experiences a miraculous event, hundreds of questions come to mind. If one is the king, one's sentiments rank considerably higher. His patience grew thin waiting for all the lovey-dovey embraces to subside. He soon interrupted.

"Riverpool!" he grunted. "You, me, now."

Legitimately, the king's heart had changed. He succumbed to the fact that if a supernatural being wanted him to get along with this hodgepodge group, then apparently it was a big deal. His heart and mind were willing, but the same discomfort filled his heart as all the rest.

Lilly's group was not quite as convinced with the king's sudden change of heart, but Lilly reassured them with the thought that Aquavita had made quite an impression upon him. She was confident, but cautious.

Lilly and the king tarried off to a small overlook of the Mirare'. The king's demeanor had certainly changed for the better. He seemed legitimate in his request to converse. His conversation started with Aquavita and eventually turned to who Lilly was and how she had found the Leaflings. A barrage of questions led to still more until, after over an hour, Lilly finally put the king in his place.

"Look, Marc, here's how I'm going to handle all this."

The king took no liking to her unkingly address but tolerated it.

"I place my trust in the Literati. I suggest you do the same. I don't know any more about the Leaflings than what you see here. We must let the Literati learn from them and teach them. They need … well … nurtured, like what Tolk suggested. They have to be near the Shard, that's all I know. Look, this time, keep the Raven lines open. I will personally see to it that you are informed of all that we do. You heard Aquavita. She said to work together. I have a feeling if we don't, she can be in our face as quickly as she chooses. I'm sure you are aware, she wins when she plays, right?"

The king nodded in agreement. "I will trust you until proven otherwise."

"I would expect no other from a valiant King." Her playful smile reassured the king, and the two parted. The king shouted over his shoulder. "I have jewels to carry. Send Ravens, Lilly Riverpool."

Lilly's father could be heard clear across the pool. He kept shouting, "I believed her! I believed her! But now, I really, REALLY believe her!"

All the while, her mother sat along the bank, rubbing her temples. "Riverpools. Mother warned me. Riverpools. But did I listen? No, no. Why, I never … life was so simple, once. Ugh!"

Elias had waited his turn. When Tolk had stated "Trust in SHE", he had no idea to what extent this would entail. Rather than take up Lilly's time at this moment, he simply stated that once back at the castle, they would spend many hours together discussing every detail to be documented.

Shark was just happy to have not drawn his sword. Seeing that a few dozen people did not come to blows was reward enough for him. He'd seen enough battle in his days over the open sea. He considered it a blessing each and every time he did not have to fight.

Ravok sat patiently on a fallen log. His one good foot swirled in the soil like a bashful kid on the playground. His painful leg was stretched before him. Lilly took note and came to his side.

"Ravok, if all trolls are supposed to be mean and ferocious, you are not living up to your calling."

Ravok was struggling with the words he pushed forward. A certain sense of guilt plagued his mind. "You know, Lilly, if you had met me before the meteor crash, I probably would have killed you. I never knew there was another way I could act. No one ever showed me kindness, and I was not about to offer it up to anyone. I'm ashamed of that, but it's true. I would have killed you, Lilly! A month ago, I would have slit your throat. I have to live with that now. Those thoughts don't enter your mind, but they do mine. I didn't deserve the aid you gave me. Yet, you did it. My soul was not worthy of saving. So why did you?"

Lilly sat down beside the enormous troll and looked up at him with a quirky smile. "You know, Rav," she stated, "my mother has taught me many things. You see, she is scared of the things she doesn't know about. It's easier for her to dislike something or someone rather than getting to know what they do or do not do. She's not mean. She just doesn't want to know. She's been taught that way, so it's only natural. You were taught to distrust. So was she. The two of you were destined to dislike one another because someone a long time ago didn't like somebody else that looked like you. It doesn't even make sense, but it happens all the time. You said that a month ago you'd have killed me. Let me tell you, a month ago, you never would have found me hiding. Even if you did, I'd have cracked both your kneecaps before you could throw your first punch. I probably would have put out your eyes before you had a chance to use brute force. Don't take all the blame, Rav. I look like a sweetie, but I have my scars, too."

Ravok took to heart what Lilly had said. It made sense to him. Aggression between peoples usually happens when one or the other aggressively forces the other to non-aggression. It's perpetual stupidity, yet it is learned behavior.

Lilly continued. "You could have killed me six different ways the day that I nursed your burns. I, too, could have defended myself in at least that many ways. We both can choose to kill or be kind. Sometimes, it's self-defense. Sometimes, it falls in our lap first. What matters is what we choose to do as the first aggressor. Me … I choose to play nice with a defense plan."

Her playful smile eased Ravok's mind. "You know, Lassy, you're too young to be so wise. Something about you could tame a Hell Wolf from the Dark Lands. These Leaflings are lucky to have you. I don't know what you are going to do with them all, though!"

"Me either, so I'm hoping Elias will come up with something."

* * *

The king and his men gathered up their tools and packed their horses. Before long, they were on their way back to Cobblestone Castle with many stories to tell.

The Leaflings were now getting to know their new friends. They scampered about like the little children that they were. After all, they were only born a few weeks ago. Given time, they would grow and evolve into their own civilization. With the help of the Literati, they would become well-schooled and highly trained in many aspects of life.

The rest of the day was spent investigating the cave behind the waterfall. The king's men had left behind many torches to aid Lilly's crew. They viewed the main tunnel reaching deep into the ground. They found numerous chambers created by the molten rock and steam. The cave would become a safe haven for the Leaflings in the years to come. It was determined by Elias that the resting place for the Shard of Amethyst should be just inside the cave entrance, hidden from view by the falling water. Elias had made many sketches of the inside of the cave for his future plans. Precautions were to be taken to ensure the safety of the Shard's resting place. Plans were made for defense should a situation arise endangering it or the Leaflings. Elias had plans to eventually build a large cross bow and other booby traps that would ensure the safety of them all.

It was settled that the Literati crew would set out in the morning for Stone Castle. Lilly and family would stay behind with the Leaflings until Elias' plans could be constructed for fortifying the cave's entrance. They would soon return with all the proper necessities for construction. Daniel was to stay behind with Lilly's family. He could read and write, which allowed notes to be sent via Tower Ravens to and from the castle. Plus, it was not likely he'd ever leave Lilly's side ever again. The two were quite inseparable.

The more pressing need fell solely on Elias. Aside from his plans for fortification of Tal Kator, he would be carrying with him the Shard of Amethyst. Knowing that the Leaflings could only endure for a couple days without it, splitting and fashioning of the stone would have to be item number one on his list in order to transport it back here as soon as possible. With the aid of the king's horse, this would be a doable plan. He would race to Stone Castle ahead of the rest and begin that process.

As night fell in Tal Kator, the moon reflected off the surface of the Mirare' as Lilly and Daniel sat side by side chatting.

"You know, Lilly," Daniel began, "I had no idea what I had gotten myself into that day I met you on the Old Road."

Lilly smiled, thinking the same. "It was your good fortune to finally meet one of the folk from the Iceland Pool."

"I'll say," he jousted. "One of those Wild Folk!"

Lilly elbowed him in his side. "There will be no more Wild talk, young man. In fact, I doubt there will be any need of talk at all." Her eyes sparkled as she said it, and she leaned in and kissed him. As she pulled him closer, a Leafling dropped into her lap. Keffer did a back flip and chanted out loud.

"Lilly! Daniel! Lilly! Daniel! Love!" He did a little cartwheel and scampered off.

Daniel took Lilly's hand.

"Yeah … Lilly, Daniel, love."

49

Elias had woken before dawn and raced away on horseback to Stone Castle. Before midday, he arrived and quickly set himself to work. The Elders followed him down into the lower halls of the castle, listening to his story as he wasted no time in starting his work.

The lower halls of Stone Castle were fascinating. Aside from the Literati's many studies, they also practiced numerous arts. Each room was dedicated to some facet of craftsmanship. One room was set for forging metalwork such as wheels and gears for odd machinery they'd fashioned. Other rooms reflected woodwork and masonry. The room Elias chose was set up for smelting precious metals and for the carving of precious stones. He would need both before he was through.

The Literati began their tedious work chipping away pieces from this glorious Amethyst stone. As they chipped and cut, every tiny piece of the stone was saved, even down to the very dust from its carving. Rather than splitting the stone as Tolk had suggested, Elias' plan was far better. He chipped and cut away ten pieces from the stone, leaving a large and beautiful, glistening purple jewel. The tiniest amount of light would illuminate the stone, casting rays all about. It was absolutely breathtaking to behold, and its energy was felt by all.

By morning, the stone had been polished and now ready for travel. Shark and his crew had arrived just after nightfall, and Shark rested for a dash back to Tal Kator on horseback with the Shard. Shark was becoming high mileage.

Elias had wrapped the stone in heavy cloth and had given Shark the explicit instruction that only the Leaflings were to unwrap it and place it within the cave. He had felt the radiant energy pulsing from the Shard, and it was all encompassing. He knew, deep inside, that the hearts and minds of men could be easily corrupted. He knew this because he had felt it himself. He found himself coveting the very stone he had sworn an oath to protect. Its energy had delved into his inner longings. He kept his emotions to himself, forever hoping the stone's secrecy could help protect it. He couldn't risk mankind feeling what he had felt in the stone. No good would come of it.

But in Elias' mind, the stone had already made its mark upon him, and he set to work on the greatest project of his life. It had to do with the remaining bits and pieces of the Shard of Amethyst.

For days, Elias carved and polished ten spectacular jewels from what was left of the Shard, saving every ounce of dust and particles from it. He then wrought and forged glorious golden rings and set the stones beautifully in place upon them. His final product was what became known to the Literati as the Amethyst Rings. They, too, had the same radiant power emitting from them as the Shard. Each ring was wrought with winding vines and leaves, paying homage to the Leaflings and their special lives.

These special rings were then given to the ten Literati Elders, who swore an oath to keep them secret and keep them safe. And without question, the Elders would do just that, for they coveted the rings as their prize possession. They were priceless to them … for many reasons.

As time would pass, the Elders felt the radiant energy pulsing from the rings. Time would prove that the rings had a glorious power for the wearer. In them, it gave life just as it had done for the Leaflings. Effectively, the rings extended the men's lives. Once worn, it would consume their hearts with a desire for the ring itself. Only in death would it be removed from the finger, and that death would be prolonged for years beyond what a human should live.

In some ways, the rings provided good things for its bearer. Aside from long life, it gave strength. It sharpened the mind. It enhanced their lives, thusly allowing them to nurture the Leaflings for decades. Had the king have known what would come of the Shard in the Literati's possession, his deeds of that day in Tal Kator may have been different. But, in the king's mind, the Leaflings did receive their Shard, and he, too, swore an oath to protect it. As far as the Literati were concerned, the world didn't need to know about the rings. It would be their secret to guard their entire lives.

And guard them, they did.

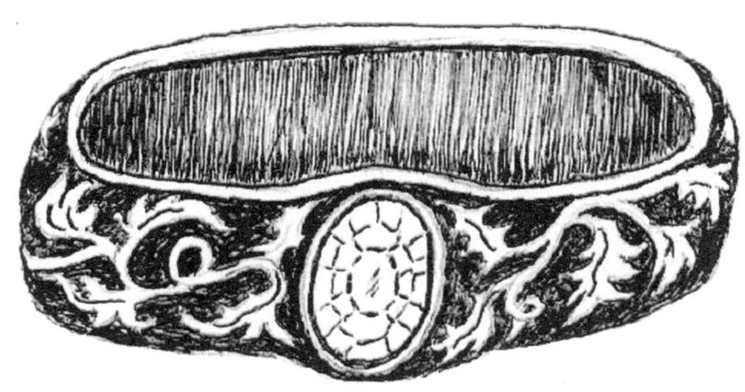

50

Time passed in the realm of Greenwale.

The king was quite pleased with the sale of many of his jewels. It allowed for the rebuilding of Cobblestone nicely, not only replacing what was lost, but upgrading many of the town's amenities. Plus, there were plenty of fine jewels left over for the queen, and when the queen is happy, everybody's happy.

The Literati implemented all the safety precautions for Tal Kator. The cave behind the falls was heavily fortified, and the Leaflings were taught the art of how to defend themselves and their precious Shard. Their schooling with the Literati gained them much knowledge, learning to speak eloquently. They had been taught to read and write early on, but that practice slowly faded. They would always prefer to teach and be taught via one another, parent to child. Their species evolved into a fine race of creatures. Of course, Lilly had a hand in it as well. Many young saplings would often ask, "Tell us, Ori, about the story of Lilly the Adventurer!"

Although Lilly's family still lived along the shores of the Iceland Pool, they spent much more time traveling to Tal Kator to spend time with the Leaflings. Lilly had given her parents and Kato a tour to see the lanterns of Cobblestone. They walked its fine streets openly, although they looked a little strange—but strangeness in the big city is quite alright. They spent many days at the Wayfarer Inn visiting with Margarite and sharing many loaves of her wonderful bread! Kato had decided that he loved the taste of bread every bit as much as Lilly. Even Lilly's mother took a liking to it. She never got up enough nerve to try pig or cow, but bread and butter was a great amendment to her diet.

Lilly and Daniel only grew deeper in love. They lived out their lives in three locations. Their home, for the most part, was Stone Castle, while many of their days were spent along the shores of the Iceland Pool. They made many trips to Blue Haven to spend time with Daniel's family, who eventually got used to the idea of their son being married to one of those Wild Folk.

Lilly and Daniel's favorite days were spent in Tal Kator. They learned the ways of the Leaflings, always enjoying their playful love of life spent near the Mirare'.

They would eventually give life to two children: a girl in their eighth year of marriage, and a boy in their tenth.

Young Margarite, as they named her, was the spitting image of her mother. She was just as playful and cunning as Lilly. She became quite worldly in her travels with her family. She had two sets of loving grandparents, and she loved her time at that wonderful Inn in Cobblestone. It was there that she'd met her namesake and promptly named her Grammy Marge. Grammie Marge took quite a liking to the little tike, considering her to truly be the grandchild she never had. In fact, Lilly's whole family was the one she never had as well. That chance meeting where she'd befriended a strange little girl from the Iceland Pool had turned out to be one of the very best actions she'd ever taken. It breathed new life into hers, and she cherished it.

Lilly and Daniel's son was more the studious type. He spent much of his time with the Literati, learning their ways and enjoying their studies. He was always the student of life, enjoying his time with the Leaflings and being a part of nature in The Deep Forest. He was given the name Mathias. He would one day age into his calling as an Elder within the Literati. In his latter years, he became High Elder of Cobblestone Abbey, but that is another story altogether.

Ravok, the troll, rarely left Tal Kator. He felt the desire to help protect that section of the forest, and he dearly loved playing with Lilly and Daniel's children. Uncle Rav must have been quite the fun brute to toy with. He found his time with that family to be healing. They helped mend his heart from his earlier days. Just after Mathias' tenth birthday, something special happened that forever changed Ravok's life. During a long journey northward near his old country, he stumbled upon another troll. She had wandered for years, feeling much the same tortures of life as he. The two would heal their hearts together and never again be lonely.

As the decades unfolded, the communities all around the realm of Greenwale would tell the stories of a courageous young girl who, through tremendous odds, introduced the world to the Leaflings. But perhaps more importantly, she was remembered for uniting many groups that would never have seen eye to eye if it weren't for her generosity and compassion. Trolls, Leaflings, animals, and mankind all had a better understanding of one another. That's a true gift to the world from a young lass named Lilly.

All because of one little girl that asked, "Why, Momma?"

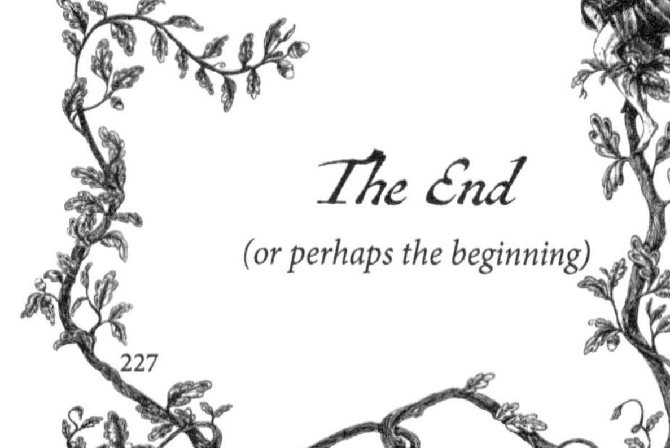

About the Author

Darren Shell has authored many works in fiction as well as compilations of historical nonfiction books about his hometown of Livingston, TN, and Dale Hollow Lake. Shell was raised on the lake and was compelled to record the lake's rich history, especially those concerning the creation of this manmade lake and its prior residents that were forced to move from their beloved homes. At the time of this writing, he still offers historical tours and ghost walks in Livingston. He resides with his wife in Allons, TN, near family and the lake that he loves. They are blessed with two children and eight grandchildren.

A note from the author:

The story of the Leaflings has been dear to me. This long and beautiful tale all stemmed from me finding the smallest little arrowhead near the lake. Those types of artifacts are referred to as bird points, but the tiny size sparked my imagination, perhaps overactive, as it may be. My time in writing the pages of my little saplings has filled my life with joy. The artwork, the creation of my stick creatures, and my time simply immersing myself in their stories has been a treasure. I offer many thanks to my editors and my readers who have offered wonderful comments and support. My publisher has nerves of steel and has created a wonder for me! Hugs to all!

www.ingramcontent.com/pod-product-compliance
Lightning Source LLC
Chambersburg PA
CBHW020610310726
48979CB00008B/1418/J

9781955622271